A ROYAL
WITHOUT RULES

A ROYAL
WITHOUT RULES

BY

CAITLIN CREWS

First published in Great Britain 2013
by Mills & Boon, an imprint of Harlequin (UK) Limited.
Large Print edition 2013
Harlequin (UK) Limited, Eton House,
18-24 Paradise Road, Richmond, Surrey TW9 1SR

© Caitlin Crews 2013

ISBN: 978 0 263 23241 7

Harlequin (UK) policy is to use papers that are natural,
renewable and recyclable products and made from
wood grown in sustainable forests. The logging and
manufacturing process conform to the legal environmental
regulations of the country of origin.

Printed and bound in Great Britain
by CPI Antony Rowe, Chippenham, Wiltshire

To Megan Haslam, who was so enthusiastic
about this book even before I wrote it,
and to Charlotte Ledger, who claimed Pato
might have ruined her for all men.

Thanks for being such fantastic editors!

CHAPTER ONE

HIS ROYAL HIGHNESS Prince Patricio, the most debauched creature in the kingdom of Kitzinia—if not the entire world—and the bane of Adriana Righetti's existence, lay sprawled across his sumptuous, princely bed in his vast apartments in the Kitzinia Royal Palace, sound asleep despite the fact it was three minutes past noon.

And he was not, Adriana saw as she strode into the room, alone.

According to legend and the European tabloids, Pato, without the pressure of his older brother's responsibilities as heir apparent, and lacking the slightest shred of conscience or propriety, had not slept alone since puberty. Adriana had expected to find him wrapped around the trollop du jour—no doubt the same redhead he'd made such a spectacle of himself with at his brother's engagement celebration the night before.

Jackass.

But as she stared at the great bed before her, the frustration that had propelled her all the way through the palace shifted. She hadn't expected to find the redhead *and* a brunette, both women naked and draped over what was known as Kitzinia's royal treasure: Prince Pato's lean and golden torso, all smooth muscle and sculpted male beauty, cut off by a sheet riding scandalously low on his narrow hips.

Although *"scandalous"* in this context was, clearly, relative.

"No need to be so shy." Somehow, Adriana didn't react to the mocking gleam in Prince Pato's gaze when she looked up to find him watching her, his eyes sleepy and a crook to his wicked mouth. "There's always room for one more."

"I'm tempted." Her crisp tone was anything but. "But I'm afraid I must decline."

"This isn't a spectator sport."

Pato shifted the brunette off his chest with a consummate skill that spoke of long practice, and propped himself up on one elbow, not noticing or not caring that the sheet slipped lower as he moved. Adriana held her breath, but the sheet *just* preserved what little remained of his modesty. The redhead rolled away from him as Pato shoved his thick, too-long tawny hair back from his forehead, amusement gleaming in eyes Adriana knew perfectly well were hazel, yet looked like polished gold.

And then he smiled with challenge and command. "Climb in or get out."

Adriana eyed him in all his unapologetic, glorious flesh. Prince Pato, international manwhore and noted black sheep of the Kitzinia royal family, was the biggest waste of space alive. He stood for nothing save his own hedonism and selfishness, and she wanted to be anywhere in all the world but here.

Anywhere.

She'd spent the last three years as Crown Prince Lenz's personal assistant, a job she adored despite the fact it had often involved handling Pato's inevitable messes. This paternity suit, that jilted lover's vindictive appearance on television, this crashed sports car worth untold millions, that reckless and/or thoughtless act making embarrassing headlines… He was the thorn in his responsible older brother's side, and therefore dug deep and hard in hers.

And thanks to his inability to behave for one single day—even at his only brother's engagement party!—Pato was now *her* problem to handle in the two months leading up to Kitzinia's first royal wedding in a generation.

Adriana couldn't believe this was happening. She'd been demoted from working at the right hand of the future king to taking out the royal family's trash. After her years of loyalty, her hard work. Just when she'd started to kid herself that she really could begin to wash away the historic stain on the once proud Righetti name.

"Pato needs a keeper," Prince Lenz had said earlier this morning, having called Adriana into his private study upon her arrival at the palace. Adriana had ached for him and the burdens he had to shoulder. She would do anything he asked, anything at all; she only wished he'd asked for something else. Pato was the one part of palace life she couldn't abide. "There are only two months until the wedding and I can't have the papers filled with his usual exploits. Not when there's so much at stake."

What was at stake, Adriana knew full well, was Lenz's storybook marriage to the lovely Princess

Lissette, which the world viewed as a fairy tale come to life—or would, if Pato could be contained for five minutes. Kitzinia was a tiny little country nestled high in the Alps, rich in world-renowned ski resorts and stunning mountain lakes bristling with castles and villas and all kinds of holiday-making splendor. Tourist economies like theirs thrived on fairy tales, not dissipated princes hell-bent on self-destruction in the glare of as many cameras as possible.

Two months in this hell, she thought now, still holding Pato's amused gaze. *Two months knee-deep in interchangeable women, sexual innuendo and his callous disregard for anything but his own pleasure.*

But Lenz wanted her to do this. Lenz, who had believed in her, overlooking her infamous surname when he'd hired her. Lenz, who she would have walked through fire for, had he wanted it. Lenz, who deserved better than his brother. Somehow, she would do this.

"I would sooner climb across a sea of broken glass on my hands and knees than into that circus carousel you call your bed," Adriana said, then smiled politely. "I mean that with all due respect, of course, Your Royal Highness."

Pato tilted back his head and laughed.

And Adriana was forced to admit—however grudgingly—that his laugh was impossibly compelling, like everything else about him. It wasn't fair. It never had been. If interiors matched exteriors, Lenz would be the Kitzinian prince who looked like this, with all that thick sun-and-chocolate hair that fell about Pato's lean face and hinted at his wildness, that sinful mouth, and the kind of bone structure that made artists and young girls weep. Lenz, not Pato, should have been the one who'd inherited their late mother's celebrated beauty. Those cheekbones, the gorgeous eyes and easy grace, the smile that caused riots, and the delighted laughter that lit whole rooms.

It simply wasn't fair.

Pato extricated himself from the pile of naked women on his bed and swung his long legs over the side, wrapping the sheet around his waist as he stood. As much to taunt her with the other women's nakedness as to conceal his own, Adriana thought, her eyes narrowing as he raised his arms high above his head and stretched. Long and lazy, like an arrogant cat. He grinned at her when she glared at him, and as he moved toward her she stiffened instinctively—and his grin only deepened.

"What is my brother's favorite lapdog doing in my bedroom this early in the day?" he asked, that low, husky voice of his no more than mildly curious. Still, his gaze raked over her and she felt a kind of clutching in her chest, a hitch in her breath. "Looking as pinch-faced and censorious as ever, I see."

"First of all," Adriana said, glancing pointedly at the delicate watch on her wrist and telling herself she wasn't *pinched* and didn't care that he thought so, "it's past noon. It's not early in the day by any definition."

"That depends entirely on what you did last night," he replied, unrepentant and amused, with a disconcerting lick of heat beneath. "I don't mean what *you* did, of course. I mean what *I* did, which I imagine was far more energetic than however it is you prepare yourself for another day of pointless subservience."

Adriana looked at him, then at the bed and its naked contents. Then back at him. She raised a disdainful eyebrow, and he laughed again, as if she delighted him. The last thing she wanted to do was delight him. If she had her way, she'd have nothing to do with him at all.

But this was not about her, she reminded herself. Fiercely.

"Second," she said, staring back at him repressively, which had no discernible effect, "it's past time for your companions to leave, no matter how energetic they may have been—and please, don't feel you need to share the details. I'm sure we'll read all about it in the papers, as usual." She aimed a chilly smile at him. "Will you do the honors or should I call the royal guard to remove them from the palace?"

"Are you offering to take their place?" Pato asked lazily.

He shifted, and despite herself, Adriana's gaze dropped to the expanse of his golden-brown chest, sun-kissed and finely honed, long and lean and—

For God's sake, she snapped at herself. *You've seen all this before, like everyone else with an internet connection.*

She'd even seen the pictures that were deemed too risqué for publication, which the palace had gnashed its collective teeth over and which, according to Lenz, had only made his shameless brother laugh. Which meant she'd seen every part of him. But she had never been this close, in person, to Prince Pato in his preferred state of undress.

It was…different. Much different.

When she forced her gaze upward, his expression was far too knowing.

"I like things my way in my bed," he said, his decadent mouth crooking into something too hot to be any kind of smile. "But don't worry. I'll make it worth your while if you follow my rules."

That crackled in the air, like a shower of sparks.

"I have no interest in your sexual résumé, thank you," Adriana snapped. She hadn't expected he'd be so *potent* up close. She'd assumed he'd repulse her—and he did, of course. Intellectually. "And in any case it's unnecessary, as it's been splashed on the cover of every tabloid magazine for years."

He shocked her completely by reaching over and tugging gently on the chic jacket she wore over her favorite pencil skirt. Once, twice, three times— and Adriana simply stood there, stunned. And let him.

By the time she recovered her wits, he'd dropped his hand, and she glanced down to see that he'd unbuttoned her jacket, so that the sides fell away and the silk of her thin pink camisole was the only thing standing between his heated gaze and her skin.

Adriana swallowed. Pato smiled.

"Rule number one," he said, his husky voice a low rumble that made her wildly beating heart pump even faster. Even harder. "You're over-dressed. I prefer to see skin."

For a moment, there was nothing but blank noise in her head, and a dangerous heat thick and bright everywhere else.

But then she made herself breathe, forcing one breath and then the next, and cold, sweet reason returned with the flow of oxygen. This was Pato's game, wasn't it? This was what he did. And she wasn't here to play along.

"That won't work," she told him coolly, ignoring the urge to cover herself. That was undoubtedly what he thought she'd do, what he wanted her to do before she ran away, screaming, like all the previous staff members Lenz had assigned him over the years. She wasn't going to be one of them.

His golden eyes danced. "Won't it? Are you sure?"

"I'm not your brother's lapdog any longer." Adriana squared her shoulders and held his gaze, tilting her chin up. "Thanks to your appalling behavior last night, which managed to deeply offend your soon-to-be sister-in-law and her entire family—to say nothing of the entire diplomatic corps—I'm yours until your brother's wedding."

If anything, Pato's eyes were even more like gold then, liquid and scalding. As wicked as he was, and her whole body seemed to tighten from the inside out.

"Really." He looked at her as if he could eat her in one bite, and would. Possibly right then and there. "All mine?"

Adriana thought her heart might catapult from her chest, and she ignored the curl of heat low in her belly, as golden and liquid as his intent gaze. *This is what he does,* she reminded herself sternly. *He's* trying *to unnerve you.*

"Please calm yourself," she said with a dry amusement she wished she felt. "I'm your new assistant, secretary, aide. Babysitter. Keeper. I don't care what you call me. The job remains the same."

"I'm not in the market for a lapdog," Pato said

in his lazy way, though Adriana thought something far more alert moved over his face for a scant second before it disappeared into the usual carelessness. "And if by some coincidence I was, I certainly wouldn't choose a little beige hen who's made a career out of scowling at me in prudish horror and ruffling her feathers in unspeakable outrage every time I breathe."

"Not when you breathe. Only when you act. Or open your mouth. Or—" Adriana inclined her head toward his naked torso, which took up far too much of her view, and shouldn't have affected her at all "—when you fling off your clothes at the slightest provocation, the way other people shake hands."

"Off you go." He made a dismissive, shooing sort of gesture with one hand, though his lips twitched. "Run back to my drearily good and noble brother and tell him I eat hens like you for breakfast."

"Then it's a pity you slept through breakfast, as usual," Adriana retorted. "I'm not going anywhere, Your Royal Highness. Call me whatever you like. You can't insult me."

"I insulted the easily offended Lissette and all of her family without even trying, or so you claim." His dark brows arched, invoking all manner of sins. Inviting her to commit them. "Imagine how offensive I could be if I put my mind to it and chose a target."

"I don't have to imagine that," Adriana assured him. "I'm the one who sorted out your last five scandals. This year."

"Various doctors I've never met have made extensive claims in any number of sleazy publications that I'm an adrenaline junkie," Pato continued, studying her, as if he knew perfectly well that the thing that curled low and tight inside her was brighter now, hotter. More dangerous. "I think that means I like a challenge. Shall we test that theory?"

"I'm not challenging you, Your Royal Highness." Adriana kept her expression perfectly smooth, and it was much harder than it should have been. "You can't insult me because, quite honestly, it doesn't matter what you think of me."

His lips quirked. "But I am a prince of the realm. Surely your role as subject and member of staff is to satisfy my every whim? I can think of several possibilities already."

How was he getting to her like this? It wasn't as if this was the first time they'd spoken, though it was certainly the longest and most unclothed inter-action she'd had with the man. It was also the only extended conversation she'd ever had with him on her own. She'd never been the focus of all his attention before, she realized. She'd only been *near* it. That was the crucial difference, and it hummed in her like an electric current no matter how little she wanted it to. She shook her head at him.

"The only thing that matters is making sure you cease to be a liability to your brother for the next two months. My role is to make sure that happens." Adriana smiled again, reminding herself that she had dealt with far worse things than an oversexed black sheep prince. That she'd cut her teeth on far more unpleasant situations and had learned a long time ago to keep her cool. Why should this be any different? "And I should warn you, Your Royal Highness. I'm very good at my job."

"And still," he murmured, his head tilting slightly to one side, "all I hear is challenge piled upon challenge. I confess, it's like a siren song to me."

"Resist it," she suggested tartly.

He gave her a full smile then, and she had the strangest sense that he was profoundly dangerous, despite his seeming carelessness. That he was toying with her, stringing her along, for some twisted reason of his own. That he was something far more than disreputable, something far less easily dismissed. It was disconcerting—and, she told herself, highly unlikely.

"It isn't only your brother who wants me here, before you ask," Adriana said quickly, feeling suddenly as if she was out of her depth and desperate for a foothold. Any foothold. "Your father does, too. He made his wishes very clear to Lenz."

Adriana couldn't pinpoint what changed, precisely, as Pato didn't appear to move. But she felt the shift in him. She could sense it in the same way she knew, somehow, that he was far more predatory than he should have been, standing there naked with a sheet wrapped around his hips and his hair in disarray.

"Hauling out your biggest weapon already?" he asked quietly, and a chill sneaked down the length of her spine. "Does that mean I've found my way beneath your skin? Tactically speaking, you probably shouldn't have let me know that."

"I'm letting you know the situation," she replied, but she felt a prickle of apprehension. As if she'd underestimated him.

But that was impossible. This was Pato.

"Far be it from me to disobey my king," he said, a note she didn't recognize and couldn't interpret in his voice. It confused her—and worse, intrigued her, and that prickle filled out and became something more like a shiver as his eyes narrowed. "If he wishes to saddle me with the tedious morality police in the form of a Righetti, of all things, so be it. I adore irony."

Adriana laughed at that. Not because it was funny, but because she hadn't expected him to land that particular blow, and she should have. She was such a fool, she thought then, fighting back a wave of a very familiar, very old despair. She should have followed her brothers, her cousins, and left Kitzinia to live in happy anonymity abroad. Why did she imagine that she alone could shift the dark mark that hovered over her family, that branded them all, that no one in the kingdom ever forgot for an instant? Why did she still persist in believing there was anything she could do to change that?

But all she showed Pato was the calm smile she'd learned, over the years, was the best response. The only response.

"And here I would have said that you'd never

have reason to learn the name of a little beige hen, no matter how long I've worked in the palace."

"I think you'll find that everybody knows your name, Adriana," he said, watching her closely. "Blood will tell, they say. And yours..." He shrugged.

She didn't know why that felt like a punch. It was no more than the truth, and unlike most, he hadn't even been particularly rude while delivering it.

"Yes, Almado Righetti made a horrible choice a hundred years ago," she said evenly. She didn't blush or avert her eyes. She didn't cringe or cry. She'd outgrown all that before she'd left grammar school. It was that or collapse. Daily. "If you expect me to run away in tears simply because you've mentioned my family's history, I'm afraid you need to prepare yourself for disappointment."

Once again, that flash of something more, like a shadow across his gorgeous face, making those lush eyes seem clever. Aware. And once again, it was gone almost the moment Adriana saw it.

"I don't want or need a lapdog," he said, the steel in his tone not matching the easy way he stood, the tilt of his head, that hot gold gleam in his eyes.

"I don't work for you, Your Royal Highness,"

Adriana replied simply, and let her profound pleasure in that fact color her voice. "You are simply another task I must complete to Prince Lenz's satisfaction. And I will."

That strange undercurrent tugged at her again. She wished she could puzzle it out, but he only gazed at her, all his shockingly intense magnetism bright in the air between them. She had the stray thought that if he used his power for good, he could do anything. Anything at all.

But that was silly. Pato was a monument to wastefulness, nothing more. A royal pain in the ass. *Her* ass, now, and for the next two months.

"I don't recall any other martyrs in the Righetti family line," he drawled after a moment. "Your people run more to murderous traitors and conniving royal mistresses, yes?" A quirk of his dark brow. "I'm happy to discuss the latter, in case you wondered. I do so hate an empty bed."

"Evidently," Adriana agreed acidly, nodding toward the overflowing one behind him.

"Rule number two," he said, sinful and dark. "I'm a royal prince. It's always appropriate to kneel in my presence. You could start right now." He nodded at his feet, though his gaze burned. "Right here."

And for a helpless moment, she imagined doing exactly that, as if he'd conjured the image inside her head. Of her simply dropping to her knees before him, then pulling that sheet away and doing what he was clearly suggesting she do.... Adriana felt herself heat, then tremble deep inside, and he smiled. He knew.

God help her, but *he knew.*

When she heard one of his bedmates call his name from behind him, Adriana jumped on it as if it was a lifeline—and told herself she didn't care that he knew exactly how much he'd got to her. Or that the curve in his wicked mouth mocked her.

"It looks like you're needed," Adriana said, pure adrenaline keeping her voice as calm and unbothered as it should have been. She knew she couldn't show him any fear, or any hint that she might waver. He was like some kind of wild animal who would pounce at the slightest hint of either—she knew that with a deep certainty she had no interest at all in testing.

"I often am," he said, a world of sensual promise

in his voice, and that calm light of too much experience in his gaze. "Shall I demonstrate why?"

She eyed the pouty redhead, who was finally sitting up in the bed, apparently as unconcerned with her nudity as Pato was.

Adriana hated him. She hated this. She didn't know or *want* to know why he'd succeeded in getting to her—she wanted to do her job and then return to happily loathing him from afar.

"I suggest you get rid of them, put some clothes on and meet me in your private parlor," she said in a clipped voice. "We need to discuss how this is going to go."

"Oh, we will," Pato agreed huskily, a dark gleam in his gaze and a certain cast to his mouth that made something deep inside her quiver. "We can start with how little I like being told what to do."

"You can talk all you want," Adriana replied, that same kick of adrenaline making her bold. Or maybe it was something else—something more to do with that odd hunger that made her feel edgy and needy, and pulsed in her as he looked at her that way. "I'll listen. I might even nod supportively. But then, one way or another, you'll behave."

* * *

Pato rid himself of his companions with as little fuss as possible, showered, and then called his brother.

"All these years I thought it was true love," he said sardonically when Lenz answered. "The descendant of the kingdom's most famous traitor and the besotted future king in a doomed romance. Isn't that what they whisper in the corners of the palace? The gossip blogs?"

There was a brief silence, which he knew was Lenz clearing whatever room he was in. Pato was happy to wait. He didn't know why he felt so raw inside, as if he was angry. When he was never angry. When he had often been accused of being incapable of achieving the state of anger, so offensively blasé was he.

And yet. He thought of Adriana Righetti and her dark brown eyes, the way she'd spoken to him. He pressed one hand against the center of his chest. Hard.

"What are you talking about?" Lenz asked, after a muttered conversation and the sound of a door closing.

"Your latest discard," Pato said. He stood there

for a moment in his dressing room, scowling at his own wardrobe. What the hell was the matter with him? He felt…tight. Restless. As if this wasn't all part of the plan. He hadn't expected her to be… *her*. "Thank you for the warning that this was happening today."

"Do you require warnings now?" Lenz sounded amused. "Has the Playboy Prince lost his magic touch?"

"I'm merely considering how best to proceed," Pato said, that raw thing in him seeming to tie itself into a knot, because he knew how he'd *like* to proceed. It was hot and raw inside him. Emphatic. "Yet all I find myself thinking about are those Righetti royal mistresses. She looks just like them. Tell me, brother, what other gifts has she inherited? Please tell me they're kinky."

"Stop!" Lenz bit out the sharp command, something Pato very rarely heard directed at him. "Have some respect. Adriana isn't like that. She never…"

But he didn't finish. And Pato blinked, everything in him going still. Too still. As if this mattered.

"Does that mean what I think that means?" he asked. It couldn't. He shouldn't care—but there was that raw thing in him, and he had to know. "Is it possible? Was Adriana Righetti, in fact, no more than your personal assistant?"

Lenz muttered a curse. "Is that so difficult to believe?"

"It defies all reason," Pato retorted. But he smiled, a deep satisfaction moving through him, and he thought of the way Adriana had looked at him, determination and awareness in her dark eyes. He felt it kick in him. Hard. "You kept her for three whole years. What exactly were you doing?"

"Working," Lenz said drily. "She happens to be a great deal more than a pretty face." He cleared his throat. "Speaking of which, the papers are having a grand time attempting to uncover the identity of your mystery woman."

"Which one?" Pato asked, still smiling.

Lenz sighed. "And still the public adores you. I can't think why."

"We all have our roles to play." He heard the restlessness in his voice then, the darkness. It was harder and harder to keep it at bay.

His older brother let out another sigh, this one tinged with bitterness, and Pato felt his own rise to the surface. Not that it was ever far away. Especially not now.

"I thought it would feel different at this point," Lenz said quietly. "I thought I would feel triumphant. Victorious. *Something.* Instead, I am nothing but an imposter."

Pato pulled on a pair of trousers and a shirt and roamed out of his dressing room, then around the great bedchamber, hardly seeing any of it. There was too much history, too much water under the bridge, and only some of it theirs. Chess pieces put in place and manipulated across the years. Choices and vows made and then kept. They were in the final stages of a very long game, with far too much at stake. Far too much to lose.

"Don't lose faith now," he said, his voice gruff. "It's almost done."

Lenz's laugh was harsh. "What does faith have to do with it? It's all lies and misdirection. Callous manipulation."

"If you don't have faith in this course of ours, Lenz," Pato said fiercely, the rawness in his brother's voice scraping inside him, "then all of this has been in vain. All of it, for all these years. And then what will we do?"

There was a muffled noise that suggested one of Lenz's aides had poked a head in.

"I must go," his brother said after another low conversation. "And this is about sacrifice, Pato, though never mine. Don't think it doesn't keep me awake, wondering at my own vanity. If I was a good man, a good brother…"

He didn't finish. What would be the point? Pato rubbed a hand over his eyes.

"It's done," he said. "The choice is made. We are who are and there's no going back."

There was a long pause, and Pato knew exactly which demons danced there between them, taunting his brother, dark and vicious. They were his, too.

"Be as kind to Adriana as you can," Lenz said abruptly. "I like her."

"We are all of us pawns, brother," Pato reminded him softly.

"Be nice to her anyway."

"Is that a command?" The raw thing in him was growing, hot and hungry. And Lenz had never touched her.

"If it has to be." Lenz snorted. "Will it work?"

Pato laughed, though it was a darker sound than

it should have been. He thought of all the moving parts of this game, all they'd done and all there was left to do before it was over. And then he thought of Adriana Righetti's sharp smile on her courtesan's mouth, then the dazed expression on her face when he'd told her to kneel. And the heat in him seemed to simmer, then become intent.

"It's never worked before," he told his brother. "But hope springs eternal, does it not?"

His certainly did.

He found Adriana waiting for him as promised in the relatively small reception room off the grandiose main foyer of his lavish palace apartment. It was filled with fussy antiques, commanding works of art and the gilt-edged glamor that was meant to proclaim his exalted status to all who entered. Pato much preferred the flat he kept in London, where he wasn't required to impart a history lesson every time a guest glanced at a chair.

She was every bit as beautiful as her famously promiscuous ancestors, Pato thought, standing in the doorway and studying her. More so. She stood at the windows that looked out over the cold, blue waters of the alpine lake surrounding the palace, impatient hands on her hips and her stiff back to the door, and there was nothing in the least bit beige about her. Or even henlike, come to that. She'd refastened her jacket, and he appreciated the line of it almost as much as he'd enjoyed ruining that line when he'd unbuttoned it earlier. It skimmed over the elegant shape of her body before flaring slightly at her hips, over the narrow sheath of the skirt she wore and the high heels that made her legs look long and lean and as if they'd fit nicely wrapped around his back.

And she had in her genetic arsenal the most celebrated temptresses in the history of the kingdom. How could he possibly resist?

Anticipation moved in him, hard and bright. He needed her with him to play out this part of the game—but he hadn't expected he'd enjoy himself. And now, he thought, he would. Oh, how he would.

There were so many ways to be nice, after all, and Pato knew every last one of them.

CHAPTER TWO

TEN DAYS LATER, Adriana stood in the middle of a glittering embassy ballroom, a serene smile pasted to her face, while inside, she itched to kill Pato. Preferably with her very own hands.

It was a feeling she was growing accustomed to the more time she spent in his presence—and the more he pulled his little stunts. Like tonight's disappearing act in the middle of a reception where he was supposed to be calmly discharging his royal duties.

Please, she scoffed inside her head, her gaze moving around the room for the fifth time, holding out hope that she'd somehow missed him before, that he'd somehow blended into a crowd for the first time in his life. *As if he has the slightest idea what the word* duty *means!*

"The prince stepped out to take an important phone call," she lied to the ambassador beside her, when she accepted, finally, what she already knew.

Pato had vanished, which could only bode ill. She kept her smile in place. "Why don't I see if I can help expedite things?"

"If you would be so kind," the ambassador murmured in reply, but without the sly, knowing look that usually accompanied any discussion of Pato or his suspicious absences in polite company. Nor did he look around to see if any women were also missing. Adriana viewed that as a point in her favor.

She had kept the paparazzi's favorite prince scandal-free for ten whole days. That was something of a record, if she did say so herself. Her intention was to continue her winning streak—but that meant finding him. And fast.

Because Adriana couldn't kid herself. She hadn't *contained* Pato over the past ten days. He'd laughed at her when she'd told him she planned to try. She'd simply babysat him, making sure he was never out of her sight unless he was asleep. That had involved frustrating days with Pato forever in her personal space, always teasing her and testing her, then doing as he pleased, with Adriana as his annoyed escort. It had meant long nights unable to sleep as she waited for the inevitable phone call from the guards she'd placed at his door to keep Pato in and the parade of trollops out. All she really had going for her was her fierce determination to bend him to her will—his brother's will, she reminded herself sternly—whether he wanted to or not.

Naturally, he didn't want to do anything of the kind.

Though he was always laughing, always shallow and reckless and the life of the party, if not the party itself, Adriana had come to realize that Pato had a fearsome will of his own. Iron and steel, wholly unbendable, beneath that impossibly pretty face and all his trademark languor.

Tonight he'd simply slipped away from the embassy receiving line, showing Adriana that he'd been indulging her this whole time. Allowing her to *think* she was making some kind of progress when, in fact, he'd been in control from the start.

She could practically *see* his mocking smile, and it burned through her, making her flush hot with the force of her temper. She excused herself from the ambassador and his aides, then walked calmly across the ballroom floor as if she was headed nowhere more interesting than the powder room, nodding by rote to those she passed and not even paying attention to the usual swell of her loathed surname like a wake of whispers behind her as she went. She was too focused on Pato, damn him.

He would *not* be the reason she failed Lenz. *He would not.*

But Pato wasn't corrupting innocents in the library, or involved in something sordid in any of the receiving rooms. She checked all of them—including every last closet because, the man was capable of anything—then stood there fuming. Had he *left?* Was he even now gallivanting about the city, causing trouble in one of the slick nightclubs he favored, filled as they were with the bored and the rich? How would she explain that to Lenz when it was all over the tabloids in the morning? But that was when she heard a soft thump from above her. Adriana tilted her head back and studied at the ceiling. The only thing above her was the ambassador's residence….

Of course. That bastard.

Adriana climbed the stairs as fast as she could without running, and then smiled at the armed guard who stood sentry at the entrance to the residence. She waved her mobile at him.

"I'm Prince Pato's assistant," she said matter-of-factly. "And I have His Majesty the King on the line…?"

She let her voice trail away, and had to fight back the rush of fury that swirled in her when the guard nodded her in, confirming her suspicions. She'd wanted to be mistaken, she really had.

And now she wanted to kill him. She *would* kill him.

Once on the other side of the ornate entryway, Adriana could hear music—and above it, a peal of feminine laughter. Her teeth clenched together, making her jaw ache. She marched down the hallway, stopped outside the cracked door where the noise came from, and then had to take a moment to prepare herself.

You already found him in bed with two women, a brisk voice inside her pointed out. *You handled it.*

She tucked her clutch beneath her arm, and wished she was wearing something more like a suit of armor, and not a sparkly blue gown that tied behind her neck, flowed to her feet and left her arms bare. For some reason, it made her feel intensely vulnerable, a sensation that mixed with her galloping temper and left her feeling faintly ill.

He was sleeping *when you saw that,* another voice countered. *He is probably not sleeping now.*

God, she hated him. She hated that this was her life. Adriana steeled herself and pushed through the door.

The music was loud, electronic and hypnotic, filling the dimly lit room. Adriana saw the woman first. She was completely naked save for a tiny black thong, plus long dark hair spilling down to the small of her back, and she was dancing.

If that was the word for it. It was carnal. Seductive. She moved to the music as if it was part of her, sensual and dark, writhing and spinning in the space between the two low couches that took up most of the floor space of the cozy room.

Performing, Adriana realized after a stunned moment. She was performing.

Pato lounged on the far couch, his long legs thrust out in front of him and crossed at the ankle, his elegant suit jacket open over his magnificent chest, and his lean arms stretched out along the back of the seat. He was fully clothed, which both surprised and oddly disappointed Adriana, but he looked no less the perfect picture of sexual indolence even though his skin wasn't showing.

Her throat went dry. The woman bent over backward, her hips circling in open, lustful invitation, her arms in the air before her. The music was like a dark throb, moving inside Adriana like a demand, a caress.

She swallowed hard, and that was when she realized Pato was looking straight at her.

Her heart stopped. Then kicked, exploding into her ribs, making her stomach drop. But Adriana didn't—couldn't—move.

The moment stretched out between them, electric and fierce. There was only that arrogant golden stare of his, as if the woman before him didn't exist. As if the music was for Adriana alone— for him. She had the panicked thought that he'd *wanted* her to find him like this, that this was some kind of trap. That he knew, somehow, the riot inside of her, the confusion. The heat.

Adriana didn't know how long she stood there, frozen on the outside and that catastrophic fire within. But eventually—seconds later? years?— Pato lifted one hand, pointed a remote toward the entertainment center on the far wall and silenced the music. All without looking away from Adriana for an instant.

The sudden silence made her flinch. Pato's mouth curved in one corner, wicked and knowing.

"It's time to go, Your Royal Highness," Adriana said stiffly into the quiet. She was aware, on some level, that the other woman was speaking, scowling at her. But Adriana couldn't seem to hear a word she said. Couldn't seem to see anything but Pato.

"You could come sit down, Adriana." His dark brows rose in challenge as he patted the sofa cushion beside him, and she was certain he knew the very moment her nipples pulled taut in a reaction she didn't understand. He smiled. "Watch. Enjoy. Who knows what might happen?"

"Not a single thing you're imagining right now, I assure you," Adriana said, struggling to control her voice.

She forced her shoulders back, stood straighter. She would not let this man best her. She couldn't let herself feel these things, whatever they were. She had too much to prove—and too much too lose. Adriana jerked her gaze away from him, ignoring his low chuckle, and frowned at the woman, who still stood there wearing nothing but a black thong and an attitude.

"Aren't you the ambassador's daughter?" she

asked sharply. "Should we call downstairs and ask your father what he thinks about your innovative approach to foreign policy?"

The woman made an extremely rude and anatomically challenging suggestion.

"No, thank you," Adriana replied coolly, unable, on some level, to process the fact that she was having this conversation while gazing at this woman's bared breasts. Not the first set of naked breasts she'd seen in Pato's company. She could only pray it was the last. "But I'm sure that if you walked into the ballroom dressed like this you'd have a few takers. No doubt that would delight your father even further."

Pato laughed then, rising from the couch with that sinuous masculine grace he didn't deserve, and straightened his suit jacket with a practiced tug. He did not look at all ashamed, or even caught out. He looked the way he always did: deeply amused. Lazy and disreputable. Unfairly sexy. His darker-than-blond hair was long enough to hint at a curl, and he wore it so carelessly, as if fingers had just or were about to run through it. That wicked mouth of his made him look like a satyr, not a prince. And those golden eyes gleamed as he held her gaze, connecting with a punch to all that confused heat inside her. Making it bloom into an open flame.

"There is no need for threats, Adriana," he said, sardonic and low, and she felt it everywhere. "Nothing would please me more than to do your bidding."

The ambassador's daughter moved then, plastering herself to his long, lean body, rubbing her naked breasts against his chest as she flung her arms around his neck, hooked one leg over his hip and pressed her mouth to his. He didn't kiss her the way Adriana had once seen him kiss one of his paramours in an almost-hidden alcove in the palace—carnal and demanding and an obvious, smoking-hot prelude to what came next. This was not *that,* thank goodness. But he didn't exactly fight her off, either.

"Then by all means, let's have you do my bidding, Your Royal Highness," Adriana said icily, everything inside her seeming to fold in on itself, like a fist. "Whenever you can tear yourself away, of course."

Pato set the other woman aside with a practiced ease that reminded Adriana of the same dexterity he'd showed in his bed that other morning. It made that fist curl tighter. Harder. He murmured something Adriana couldn't hear, that made the ambassador's thonged daughter smile at him as if he'd licked her. And then he smoothed down his tie, buttoned his jacket and sauntered toward the doorway as if there wasn't a nearly naked woman panting behind him and a formal reception he was supposed to be attending below.

Adriana stepped back to let him move into the hallway, and took more pleasure than she should have in snapping the door shut behind him. Perhaps with slightly more force than necessary.

"Temper, temper," Pato murmured, eyeing her with laughter in that golden gaze. "And here I thought you'd be so proud of me."

"I doubt you thought anything of the kind." She'd never wanted to hit another human being so much in all her life. "I doubt you *think*. And why on earth would I be proud of this embarrassing display?"

He propped one shoulder against the closed door and waved a languid hand down the length of him, inviting her to take a long look. She declined. Mostly.

"Am I not clothed?" he asked, taunting her. Again. "'Keep your clothes on, Your Royal Highness,' you said in that prissy way of yours in the car on the way over tonight. I am delighted, as ever, to obey."

"You wouldn't know how to *obey* if it was your job," she snapped at him. "Not that I imagine you know what one of those is, either."

"You make a good point," he said, and that was when it occurred to Adriana that they hadn't moved at all—that they were standing entirely too close in that doorway. His face shifted from pretty to predatory, and her head spun. "I'm better at giving the orders, it's true. Rule number three, Adriana. The faster you obey me, the harder and the longer you'll come. Consider it my personal guarantee."

She couldn't believe he'd said that. Her entire body seemed to ignite, then liquefy.

"Enough," she muttered, but she didn't fool him with her horrified tone, if that flash of amused satisfaction in his gaze meant anything. Desperation made her lash out. "You shouldn't share these sad rules of yours, Your Royal Highness. It only makes you that much more pathetic—the dissipated, aging bachelor, growing more pitiable by the moment, on a fast track to complete irrelevance."

"Yes," he agreed. He leaned closer, surrounding

her, mesmerizing her. "That's exactly why you're breathing so fast, why your cheeks are so flushed. You pity me."

Adriana ducked around him and started down the hall, telling herself none of that had happened. None of it. No dancing girl, no strange awareness. No *rules* that made her belly feel tight and needy. And certainly not the look she'd just seen in his eyes, stamped hard on his face. But her heart clattered in her chest, it was as hard to breathe as he'd suggested, and she knew she was lying.

Worse, he was right beside her.

"You're welcome," Pato said after a moment, sounding smug and irritatingly male. It made her pulse race, but she refused to look at him. She couldn't seem to stop herself from imagining what kind of orders he'd give…and she hated herself for wondering.

"I beg your pardon?" she asked icily, furious with herself.

"Someone needs to provide fodder for your fantasies, Adriana. I live to serve."

She stopped walking, her hand on the door that led out of the residence. When she looked at him, she ignored the impact of that hot golden gaze of his and smiled instead. Poisonously.

"My fantasies involve killing you," she told him. "I spend hours imagining burying you in the palace gardens beneath the thorniest rose bushes, so I'd never have to deal with you again." She paused, then added with exaggerated politeness, "Your Royal Highness."

Pato grinned widely, and leaned down close. Too close. Adriana was aware, suddenly and wildly, of all the skin she was showing, all of it *right there,* within his reach. All that bare flesh, so close to that satyr's mouth of his. That wicked mouth with a slight smear of crimson on it, a sordid little memento that did nothing to detract from his devastating appeal. Or from her insane response to him.

"I knew you fantasized about me," he murmured, his voice insinuating, delicious. Seductive. "I can see it on your face when you think it's not showing."

He ran his fingertip down the sparkling blue strap that rose from the bodice of her gown and fastened at the nape of her neck. That was all. That was enough. He touched nothing but the fabric, up and down and back again, lazy and slow and so very nearly innocuous.

And Adriana burned. And shivered. And hated herself.

"Someday," he whispered, his eyes ablaze, "I'll tell you what you do in my fantasies. They're often…complicated."

Adriana focused on that smear of lipstick on his perfect lips. She didn't understand any of this. She should be horrified, disgusted. She should find him categorically repulsive. Why didn't she? What was *wrong* with her?

But she was terrified that she already knew.

"That's certainly something to look forward to," she said, the deliberate insincerity in her voice like a slap, just as she'd intended, but he only grinned again. "In the meantime, you have lipstick all over your mouth." She kept her expression smooth as she stepped back, away from him. She snapped open her clutch, reached inside with a hand that was *not* shaking, and produced a tissue. "I know you like to trumpet your conquests to all and sundry but not, I beg you, tonight. Not the ambassador's daughter."

"They wouldn't think it was the ambassador's

daughter who put her mouth all over me, Adriana." He held her with that golden stare for another ageless moment, so sure of himself. So sure of *her*. He took the tissue from her hand then, his fingers brushing over hers—leaving nothing behind but heat and confusion, neither of which she could afford. "Small minds prefer the simplest explanations. They'd assume it was you."

"You must have done *something*," Adriana's father said peevishly, and not for the first time. "I told you to ingratiate yourself, to be obliging, didn't I? I told you to be careful!"

"You did," Adriana agreed. She didn't look over at her mother, who was preparing breakfast at the stove. She didn't have to look; she could feel her mother's sympathy like a cool breeze through the room. She tried to rub away the tension in her temples, the churning confusion inside her. "But I didn't do anything, I promise. Lenz thinks this is a great opportunity for me."

There was a tense silence then, and Adriana blinked as she realized her mistake. Her stomach twisted.

"'*Lenz?*'" Her father's brows clapped together.

"You're quite familiar with the crown prince and future king of Kitzinia, are you not? I don't need to tell you where that leads, Adriana. I don't need to remind you whose blood runs through your veins. The shame of it."

He didn't. He really didn't, as she was the one who lived it in ways he couldn't imagine, being male. But he always did, anyway. She could see that same old lecture building in him, making his whole body stiffen.

"Papa," she said gently, reaching over to cover his hands with hers. "I worked with him for three years. A certain amount of familiarity is to be expected."

"And yet he insults you like this, throwing you to his dog of a brother like refuse, straight back into the tabloids." Her father frowned at her, and a small chill tickled the back of her neck. "Perhaps his expectation was for rather more familiarity than you offered, have you thought of that?"

It wasn't the first time her father had managed to articulate her deepest fears. But this time it seemed to sting more. Adriana pulled her hands away.

"Eat, Emilio," her mother said then, slipping into her usual seat and raising her brows when Adriana's father only scowled at the cooked breakfast she set before him. "You hate it when your eggs get cold."

"It was never like that," Adriana said, pushed to defend herself—though she wasn't sure she was addressing her father as much as herself. "Lenz is a good man."

"He is a man," her father replied shortly, something she didn't like in his gaze. "A very powerful man. And you are a very beautiful woman with only a terrible history and a disgraced family name to protect you."

"Emilio, please," her mother interjected.

Her father looked at her for an uncomfortable moment, then dropped his gaze to his meal, his silence almost worse. Adriana excused herself, unable to imagine eating even a bite when her stomach was in knots.

She made her way through the ancient villa to her childhood bedroom. It would be easier to leave Kitzinia altogether, she knew. She'd sat up nights as a child, listening to her mother beg her father to emigrate, to live in a place where their surname need never cause any kind of reaction at all. But Emilio Righetti was too proud to abandon the country his ancestor had betrayed, and Adriana understood it, no matter how hard it was to bear sometimes, no matter how she wished she didn't. Because when it came right down to it, she was the same.

She shut the door to her bedroom behind her and sank down on the edge of her bed. She was so tired, though she didn't dare let herself sleep. She had to return to the palace. Had to face Pato again.

Adriana let her eyes drift shut, wishing herself far away from the villa she'd grown up in, surrounded by the remains of the once vast Righetti wealth. If she looked out her window, she could see the causeway the kingdom had built in the 1950s, linking the red-roofed, picturesque city that spread along the lakeside to the royal palace that sat proudly on its own island in the middle of the blue water, its towers and spires thrust high against the backdrop of the snowcapped Alps. The villa boasted one of the finest addresses in the old city, a clear indication that the Righettis had once been highly favored by many Kitzinian rulers.

Now the villa was a national landmark. A reminder. The birthplace and home of the man who had murdered his king, betrayed his country, nearly toppling the kingdom with his treachery. Because of him, all the rest of the Righetti family history was seen through a negative lens. There had been other royal mistresses from other noble Kitzinian families—but only the Righettis enjoyed the label of witches. Whores.

There was no escape from who she was, Adriana knew. Not as long as she stayed here. And she didn't understand what was happening to her now—what was happening *in* her. What had ignited in her last night at that embassy party under Pato's arrogant golden stare. What had stalked her dreams all through the long night, erotic and wild, and still thrummed beneath her skin when she woke...

That was a lie, she thought now, cupping a hand over the nape of her neck as if she could ease the tension she felt. Adriana knew exactly what was happening. She didn't *want* to understand it, because she didn't want to admit it. Yet the way her father had looked at her today, as if she was somehow visibly tainted by the family history, made it impossible to keep lying to herself.

She'd heard it all her life. It had been flung at her in school and was whispered behind her back even now. It wasn't enough that she was assumed to be traitorous by blood, like all her male relatives. She was the only female Righetti of her generation, and more, was the very image of her famous forebears—there were portraits in the Royal Gallery to prove it. They were well-known and well-documented whores, all the way down to Adriana's great-aunt, who had famously beguiled one of the king's cousins into walking away from his dukedom, disowned and disgraced.

And Adriana was just like them.

She knew exactly how tainted she really was, how very much she lived down to her family's legacy. Because it wasn't Lenz who had dreamed of something more familiar. It was her.

Lenz was good and kind, and he'd believed in her. He'd given her a chance. Adriana was the first Righetti to set foot in the palace since her traitorous ancestor had been executed there a hundred years ago, and Lenz had made that happen. He'd changed everything. He'd given her hope. And in return, Adriana had adored him, happy simply to be near him.

And yet she'd dreamed of Pato in ways she'd never dreamed of his brother. Wild and sensual.

Explicit. Maybe it shouldn't surprise her that she couldn't get Pato out of her head, she thought now in a wave of misery. Maybe it was programmed into her very flesh, her bones, to want him. To want anything, anyone royal, moving from one prince to the next. To be exactly what she'd always been: a Righetti.

That was what they said in the tabloids, which had pounced on her switch from Lenz's office to Pato's with malicious glee, after three years of going a bit easier on her. *She's failed to snare Prince Lenz with her Righetti wiles—will the shameless Pato be easier to trap?*

Maybe this had all been inevitable from the start.

Her mobile phone chirped at her from the bedside table, snapping her eyes open. She reached for it and tensed when she saw the name that flashed on the screen. It felt like confirmation that she was cursed. But she picked it up, because Pato was her job. Her responsibility. It didn't matter what she felt.

It only mattered what she did, and she controlled that. Not him. Not the ghosts of her slutty ancestors. Not her own treacherous blood.

Stop being so melodramatic, she ordered herself, pulling in a deep breath. *Nothing is inevitable.*

"It's eight-fifteen in the morning," she said by way of a greeting, and she didn't bother to sweeten her tone. "Surely too early for your usual debauchery."

"Pack your bags," Pato said, sounding uncharacteristically alert despite the hour. "We're flying to London this afternoon. There's some charity thing I had no intention of attending, and now, apparently, must. My brother commands it."

Adriana blinked, and sorted through the possibilities in her head.

"Presumably you mean the Children's Foundation, of which you and your brother are major benefactors," she said crisply. "And their annual ball."

"Presumably," he agreed, that alertness blending into his more typical laziness, and prickling over her skin no matter how badly she didn't want to be affected. "I don't really care, I only follow orders. And Adriana?"

"Yes?" But she knew. She could hear it in his voice. She could imagine that smile in the corner of his mouth, that gleam in his eyes. She didn't have to see any of it—she felt it. Her eyes drifted shut again, and she hated herself anew.

"It's never too early for debauchery," he said in that low, stirring way that was only his. "I'd be delighted to prove that to you. You can make it back to the palace in what? Twenty minutes?"

"You need to stop," she retorted, not realizing she meant to speak, and then it sat there between them. Pato didn't reply, but she could *feel* him. That disconcerting power of his, that predatory beauty. She dropped her forehead into one hand, kept her eyes shut. "I'm not your toy. I don't expect you to make my job easy for me, but this is unacceptable." He still didn't speak, but she could feel the thrum of him inside her, the electricity. "Not every woman you meet wants to sleep with you."

He laughed, and she felt it slide through her like light, illuminating too many truths she'd prefer to hide away forever. Exposing her. Making that curl of heat glow again, low and hot, proving what a liar she was.

"Rule number four," he began.

"Would you like to know what you can do with your rules?" she demanded, desperate.

"Adriana," he chided her, though she could hear

the thread of laughter in his voice. Somehow, that made it worse. "I'm fairly certain I could legally have you beheaded for speaking to me in such an appalling fashion, given the medieval laws of our great kingdom. I am your prince and your employer, not one of your common little boyfriends. A modicum of respect, please."

She was too raw. Too unbalanced. It crossed her mind then that she might not survive him. Certainly not intact. That he might be the thing that finally broke her.

"I apologize, Your Royal Highness," she said, her voice much too close to a whisper. "I don't know what came over me."

"Rule number four," he said again, softly. And meanwhile her heart thudded so hard in her chest that she could feel the echo of it in her ears, her teeth. Her sex. "If you can't muster up the courage to say it to my face, I'm not going to take it seriously."

Because he knew, of course. That she was using this phone conversation to hide, because she doubted her own strength when he was standing in front of her. He'd watched it, hadn't he? Exploited it. He knew exactly how weak she was.

And now she did, too.

"London," she said, changing the subject, because she had to end this conversation right now. She had to find her balance again, or at least figure out how to fake it. "A charity ball. I'll pack appropriately, of course."

"Say it to my face, Adriana," he urged her, and she told herself she didn't recognize what she heard in his voice then. But her skin broke out in goose bumps, even her breasts felt heavy, and she knew better. She knew. "See what happens."

"I should be back in the palace within the hour, Your Royal Highness," she said politely, and hung up.

And then sat there on the edge of her bed, her head in her hands, and wondered what the hell would become of her if she couldn't find a way to control this. To control *herself.*

Because she was terribly afraid that if she couldn't, Pato would.

CHAPTER THREE

THE CHARITY BALL in London was, of course, as tedious as every other charity ball Pato had ever attended. He smiled. He posed for obligatory photographs with Lenz and the chilly Lissette, as well as with any number of other people whose names he forgot almost before he heard them. He then contemplated impaling himself on the dramatic ice sculpture near the lavish buffet to see if that might enliven the evening in some small way.

"Restrain yourself," Adriana replied, in that stuffy voice that he found amused him far more than it should, when he announced his intentions. Pato angled a look at her.

She stood beside him as she had all evening, never more than three steps away, as if she'd put him on an invisible leash and was holding it tight. Her lovely face was smoothed to polite placidity, she knew exactly how to blend into the background whenever someone came to speak to him, and she held her mobile phone tight in one hand as if she planned to use it to subdue him if he made a break for it. She'd been nothing but irritatingly serene and unflappably professional since she'd returned to the palace with her packed bag this morning. And all this time, across the span of Europe and the whole of London, she'd managed to avoid looking at him directly.

Pato found her fascinating.

"Restraint?" he asked, noting the way her shoulders tensed beneath the cap sleeves of the elegant black sheath she wore when he spoke. Every time he spoke. It made him want to press his mouth to her collarbone, to lick his way up the curve of her neck to the subdued sparkle of small diamonds at her ears. "I'm unfamiliar with the concept."

She smiled slightly, but kept her attention trained on the dance floor in front of them. "Truer words have never been spoken, Your Royal Highness."

He laughed. He liked it when she slapped at him, when her voice was something more than cool, smooth, bland. He liked when he could sense her temper, her frustration. He found that the more he told her how bored he was, the less bored he actually felt.

Pato knew he was on dangerous ground. He didn't care. He hadn't enjoyed himself so much in years.

A curvy brunette in a slinky dress slithered up to him then, her heavily kohled eyes sweeping over Adriana dismissively before she leaned in close and ran her hands over Pato's chest.

"Your Royal Highness," she purred, her lips painted a sultry red that matched the fingernails she ran along the length of his tie. "We meet again. I knew we would."

Pato smiled indulgently. He had no idea who she was. "And you were right."

Beside him, he felt Adriana bristle, and he enjoyed that immensely, so he picked up the brunette's hand and kissed it, making her lean even more heavily against him.

"Dance with me," she commanded him in a sultry voice.

Pato didn't feel like dancing and he wasn't particularly fond of commands, but he could feel Adriana's disapproval like a cold wind at his back, and so he smiled wider.

"I'm afraid I'm here with my own version of an electronic ankle bracelet," he said blithely, turning slightly. He indicated Adriana with a nod of his head, and was pleased to notice she flushed. At the attention? Or was that the sweet kick of her temper? And why did he want so badly to know? "It's like a walking house arrest."

The brunette blinked, looking from him to Adriana and then back.

"What did you do?" she asked, wide-eyed, no doubt plotting her call to the tabloids as she spoke.

"Haven't you heard?" Pato asked, his eyes on Adriana and the way her hand tensed around her mobile as she glared out at the crowd. "I've been very, very naughty. Again."

The brunette made some reply, but Pato watched Adriana, who dragged her gaze to his then as if it hurt her to do it. Even better, her meltingly brown eyes shot fire at him.

"There you are," he said quietly, with a satisfaction he didn't bother to hide. He smiled when her eyes narrowed. He tried to make his voice sound like a supplicant's, but what came out was more like lazy challenge. "Am I allowed to dance, Adriana? Is that permitted?"

"Stay where I can see you," she ordered him, all smooth command, as if she really did have him under her control. His smile deepened when she turned a cool gaze on the brunette. "Please don't force me to invoke Kitzinian law, ma'am. No leaving the ballroom. No public displays. Keep it clean and polite. Do you understand?"

The woman nodded, looking slightly dazed, and Pato laughed.

"My very own prison warden," he said, as if he approved. "I am duly chastened."

He pulled the brunette into his arms as he took to the floor, but he couldn't seem to take his eyes off Adriana, who stood where he'd left her, looking calm and unruffled. Serene. She even gazed at him across the swell of bodies, a kind of victory in her dark eyes. He felt it like a direct challenge.

When the interminable dance was finished, he murmured the appropriate things to the brunette, forgot her and then prowled back over to the assistant he'd never wanted in the first place. This time, she looked at him as he approached. More than that, she met his eyes boldly. He didn't know why that should affect him far more than the way the lush brunette had leaned against him throughout the dance, trying to entice him with her curves.

"You don't know who that woman is, do you?"

Adriana asked when he reached her side, her tone mild. Polite. Pato knew better than to believe it.

"I haven't the faintest idea."

"But you slept with her." Something like panic flared in her dark gaze, intriguing him even as she blinked it away. The tips of her ears were red, he noticed, up there near her swept-back blond hair, and her eyes were too bright. "Didn't you?"

"Probably." He arched a brow at her. "Are you asking that in an official capacity, Adriana? Or are you jealous?"

"I'm merely curious," she said with a sniff, sounding as if she was discussing something as dry and uninteresting as his daily schedule. "I imagine, at this point, you can't walk across a single room in Europe without tripping over legions of former conquests."

"Well," he said. "I rarely trip."

"It must be difficult, at this point, to find someone you *haven't* already been intimate with." She smiled at him, that killer smile he'd seen before, sweet and deadly, which was supposed to be a weapon and instead delighted him. "Then again, it's not as if you can remember, anyway, can you?"

Pato stood there for a moment, that same jagged

restlessness beating at him, making him want things he'd given up a long time ago. Making him hard and wild, and shoving him much too close to a line he couldn't allow himself to cross.

And still she smiled at him like that, as if she could handle this kind of battle, when he knew she was completely unaware of how much danger she was in.

"Ah," he said in the low voice he could see made her shiver, and then he smiled as if she was prey and he was already on her. In her. "I see." And he was closer than he should have been. He was much too close and he didn't care at all, because her eyes widened and were that intoxicating shade of the finest Swiss chocolate. "You're under the impression that you can shame me."

They stared at each other, while laughter and conversation and the music kicked around them. Her lovely face flushed red. He saw the flash of that same panic he'd seen before, as if she wasn't at all as controlled as she pretended, but she didn't look away. Brave, he thought. Or foolish.

Pato lost himself in her dark gaze then, electric and alive and focused on him as if nothing else existed. As if he was already buried deep inside her, and she was waiting for him to move.

That image didn't help matters at all. He blew out a breath.

"Come," he said shortly, annoyed with himself. He turned on his heel and started across the great ballroom, knowing she had no choice but to follow, to keep him on that absurd leash of hers. And she did.

"Where are you going?" she asked as she fell into step with him. He didn't think that hint of breathlessness in her voice was from walking, and it carved out something like a smile inside him.

"It's like we're chained together, Adriana." He couldn't seem to find his footing, and that was a catastrophe waiting to happen. And still, he didn't care about that the way he knew he should. "Think of the possibilities."

"No, thank you," she replied, predictably, and he indulged himself and wrapped his hand around her upper arm, feigning solicitousness as he moved her through the door that led out toward the gardens. She jumped when he touched her, electric shock and that darker kick beneath it. He knew because he felt it, too. Her skin was softer than satin, warm and smooth beneath his palm, she smelled faintly of jasmine, and he shouldn't have done it. Because now he knew.

Her eyes flew to his, and it punched through him hard, making him want to push her back against the nearest wall, lift her against him, lose himself completely in the burn of it. In her.

"Are you sure?" he asked, as they moved from the bright light of the ballroom into the soft, cool dark outside. He led her across the wide patio, skirting the small clumps of people who stood clustered around the bar tables that dotted it here and there. "Five minutes ago my sexual escapades were foremost on your mind. Don't tell me you've lost interest so quickly."

He looked down at her, and made no effort to contain the heat in him. The fire. He felt a tremor run through her, and God help him, he wanted her more than he'd wanted anything in years.

"I didn't realize you were so sensitive about your scandalous past, Your Royal Highness," she said, in a rendition of her usual cool he might have believed, had he not been looking into the wild heat in her gaze. "I'll take care not to mention it again."

"Somehow," he murmured, his grip on her

arm tightening just enough to make her suck in a breath, just enough to torture himself, "I very much doubt that."

At some point, he was going to have to figure out why this woman got to him like this. But not tonight. Not now.

She pulled her arm from his grip as he steered her between two tables, as if concerned they couldn't make it through the narrow channel side by side. But she rubbed at the place he'd touched her as if he'd left behind a mark, and Pato smiled.

In the deepest, farthest shadows of the patio, he found an empty table, the candle in the center, which should have been glowing, unlit. But he didn't need candlelight to see her as she deliberately put the table between them, keeping as far out of his reach as she could. His eyes adjusted to the dark and he studied the flush on her cheeks, the hectic sparkle in her gaze.

And then he waited, leaning his elbows on the table and watching her. Her pretty eyes widened. She shifted from one foot to the other. He made her nervous, and he couldn't pretend he didn't like it.

"I wasn't trying to shame you," she said after long moments passed, just the two of them in a far, dark corner, all the nerves he could see on her face rich in her voice. And there was something else, he thought as he studied her. Something he couldn't quite identify.

"Of course you were."

"I didn't mean—"

"You did."

She looked stricken for a moment, then dropped her gaze to the tabletop, and he watched as she crossed her arms as if she thought she needed to hold herself together. Or protect herself.

"What are you ashamed of, Adriana?" he asked softly.

She flinched as if he'd slapped her, telling him a great deal more than he imagined she meant to do, but her expression was clear when she lifted her head. That mask again. She let out a breath and then she opened her mouth—

"Don't lie to me," he heard himself say, and worse, he could feel how important it was to him that she heed him. How absurdly, dangerously important. "Don't clean it up. Just tell me."

"I'm a Righetti, Your Royal Highness," she said after a moment, her dark eyes glittering in the shadows. "Shame runs like blood in our veins. It's who we are."

Pato didn't know how long they stood like that, held in that taut, near-painful moment. He didn't know how long he gazed at her, at the proud tilt of her chin and the faintest tremor in her lips, with that darkness in her eyes. He didn't know how she'd punched into him so completely that her hand might as well have ripped through his chest. That was what it felt like, and he didn't want that. He didn't want *this.* He couldn't.

"Adriana," he said finally, but his voice was no more than a rasp. And then he saw figures approaching from the corner of his eye, and he stopped, almost grateful for the intrusion into a moment that shouldn't have happened in the first place.

She dropped her gaze again, and hunched her shoulders slightly as she stood there, as if warding off whoever had come to stand at the table a small distance behind her. Pato didn't spare them a glance. He didn't look away from Adriana for even a moment, and the fact that was more dangerous than anything that had come before didn't escape him.

He wanted to touch her. He wanted to pull her against him, hold her, soothe her somehow, and he felt hollow inside because of it. Hollow and twisted, and stuck where he'd put himself, on the other side of an incidental table and an impossible divide, useless and corrupt and dismissable.

A fine bed he'd made, indeed.

And then she stiffened again, as if she'd been struck, and Pato frowned as he recognized the voices coming from behind her.

"Was that wise, do you think?" The cold, precise tones of Princess Lissette, her faint accent making the words seem even icier. She sounded as blonde and Nordic as she looked, Pato thought uncharitably. And as frigid.

"I'm not sure what wisdom has to do with it."

There was no mistaking his brother's voice, and the ruthlessly careful way he spoke while in public. The dutiful Crown Prince Lenz and his arranged-since-the-cradle bride stood at the next table, a candle bright between them, the warm glow doing nothing to ease their stiff, wary postures.

There were worse beds to lie in than his, Pato knew, eyeing his brother. *Poor bastard.*

"One must strive to be compassionate, of course,"

Lissette continued in the same measured way. "But even I know of her family's notoriety. Do you worry that it reflects badly on your judgment, your discernment, that you selected her to be your assistant when she is widely regarded as something of a pariah?"

Pato went still. Adriana seemed turned to stone, a statue, her eyes lowered as she bent slightly forward over her crossed arms.

"Look at me," he ordered her in an undertone, but she ignored him.

Behind her, an uncomfortable silence swelled. Pato saw his brother begin to frown, then remember himself and fight it back. His ice princess fiancée only gazed back at him calmly. Pato wanted to order them to stop talking, to point out that Adriana was *right here*—but he didn't trust that the princess would stop. Or that she wasn't already aware that Adriana stood at the next table. And he didn't want Adriana to be any more of a target. A dim alarm sounded in him then, questioning that unusual protective urge, but he shoved it aside.

"This will all go much smoother, I think," Lenz said finally, an edge to his voice, "if you do not speak of things you don't understand, Princess."

"I believe I understand perfectly," she replied with cool hauteur. "You took a traitor's daughter as your mistress and flaunted her in the face of Kitzinian society, for years. What is there to misunderstand?"

"Adriana Righetti was never my mistress," Lenz snapped, his tone scathing. Even derisive. "Credit me with slightly more intelligence than that, Lissette."

There were other voices then, calling out for the happy royal couple from some distance across the patio, and Pato watched in a quiet fury as his brother pasted on his usual public smile, offered his arm to his fiancée—who smiled back in the same way as she took it—before they glided away. He had the wholly uncharacteristic urge to smack their heads together.

Then he glanced back at Adriana, who still hadn't moved a muscle.

"Look at me," he said again, with an odd urgency he didn't understand.

She lifted her head then and the pain on her face stunned him into silence. He could see it in her dark eyes, slicked not with embarrassment but with a kind of grief.

For a moment he was lost. This wasn't the tough, impervious Adriana he'd grown accustomed to over the past days—unflappable, he'd assumed, thanks to growing up a beautiful Righetti girl in the sharp teeth of Kitzinian society. But then, suddenly, he understood.

And didn't care at all for how it made him feel.

"My God," he said flatly. "You're in love with him."

Adriana woke up in a rush and had no idea where she was.

She was on her stomach on an unfamiliar bed in a sunlit room she'd never seen before. She blinked, frowned, and realized as she did both that her head ached and that she'd neglected to remove her eye makeup the night before. What—

There was a slight movement behind her, a small shift against the mattress.

She was not alone in the bed.

Adriana froze. Then, very slowly, her heart pounding, she turned to look, somehow knowing what she would see even as she prayed she was mistaken.

Please not him. Please not him. Please—

Prince Pato lay sprawled out on his back, the sheets kicked off, naked save for a pair of tight navy blue briefs that clung to his narrow hips. The light from the skylights bathed him in shades of gold, and she couldn't quite take in that perfect, hard-packed flesh of his, so close beside her she could almost feel the heat he generated, and could see the rough shadow of his beard on his jaw. She couldn't make sense of all his fine masculine beauty, much less the picture of sheer abandon he made, sun-kissed and golden and stretched out so carelessly against the crisp white sheets.

She was in bed with Pato.

Her mouth was too dry; her eyes felt scraped and hollow. She felt fragile and broken, and had no idea how to pull herself together enough to handle this. Adriana was afraid she might be sick.

In a panic, she whipped her head around, yanked back the sheet and looked down at herself, not sure whether to be horrified or relieved to discover that while she wasn't naked, she wore only the matching cranberry hip-slung panties and bra she'd had on beneath her gown at the charity ball.

The ball. Adriana fought to keep breathing as images from the night before began to flood her head. Those strange, intense moments with Pato. His hand on her arm. The way he'd looked at her, as if he could see straight into her. Then Lenz's voice, so disgusted, so appalled.

She couldn't think about Lenz. She couldn't.

Had she really done this? Had she decided to become what she'd always been so proud she wasn't? With the one person in all the world best suited to debauch her—or anyone, come to that—completely? He did it by rote, no doubt. He could do it in his sleep. No wonder she couldn't recall it.

Adriana turned to look at him again, as if she might see her own actions tattooed on his smooth skin, and she jolted in shock.

Pato was awake. And watching her.

"Oh, my God," she whispered. She pulled the sheets up to her neck, fought the urge to burst into tears, and stared at him in horror.

Pato's golden eyes were sleepy, his hair a thick, careless mess, and still he fairly oozed the same sensual menace he had the night before, when he'd been dressed so elegantly. He studied her for a long moment, and the great, wide bed felt like a tiny little cot, suddenly. Like a trap. Adriana's pulse beat at her, and she forgot about her headache.

"I hope you appreciate the sacrifice I made to your modesty," Pato said in that drawling way of his, as if he was too lazy to bother enunciating properly. He waved at the form-fitting briefs he wore. At that flat abdomen of his, the crisp dark hair that disappeared beneath the fabric. She jerked her eyes away, and his mouth curved. "I think you know very well I prefer to sleep naked."

Adriana felt dizzy, and part of her welcomed it. Encouraged it. It would be such a relief to simply faint dead away. To escape whatever morning-after this was. She lifted a hand to her head, only belatedly realizing that her hair had tumbled down from its chignon, and was hanging around her face in a wild mess that rivaled Pato's.

Somehow, that made it worse. It made her feel like the wanton slut she must have become last night. Was it possible to share a bed with Prince Pato and *not* be a wanton slut? Her chest felt tight.

He watched her as she pushed the mass of blond waves behind her shoulders, his golden gaze like a flame as it touched her. More images from the previous night flashed through her head then, as if the heat of his gaze triggered her memory, and she frowned at him.

"You got me drunk," she accused him.

Blaming him felt good. Clean. Far better to concentrate on that and not the images flickering in her head. Some dark-paneled pub, or possibly the kind of rich man's club a prince might frequent, thick with reds and woods and the shots of strong spirits Pato slid in front of her, one after the next, his golden gaze never leaving her face. His elegant hands brushing hers. That wicked mouth of his much too close.

"You got you drunk," he corrected, shifting over to his side and propping his head up on one hand as he continued to regard her with that lazy intent that made her belly fold in on itself. "Who was I to stand in your way?"

A dark street, laughter. *Her* laughter, and the wicked current of his voice beneath it. Her arm around Pato's waist and his lean, hard arm around her shoulders. Then being held high against his chest as he moved through some kind of lobby…

This was awful, Adriana thought then, her chest aching with the sobs, the screams, she refused to let out. This was beyond awful.

"My God." She said it again, despite the decided lack of any divine intervention this morning. She squeezed her eyes shut, bracing herself for the blow. Preparing herself, because she had to know. "Did you—? Did we—?"

There was nothing but silence. Adriana dared to open her eyes again, to find that Pato was staring at her in outrage.

She shuddered. "Does that mean we did?" she asked in a tiny voice.

"First of all," he said, in that low voice of his that curled around her like a caress, and she couldn't seem to shake it off, "I am not in the habit of taking advantage of drunk women who pretend to detest me when they are sober, no matter how much they beg."

His gaze was hard on hers, and Adriana felt caught in the heat, the command, that surely a wastrel like Pato shouldn't have at his disposal. Eventually, his mouth moved into a small, sexy grin that shouldn't have tugged at her like that, all fire and need in the core of her, then a shiver everywhere else. She couldn't seem to think, to move. To breathe. She could only stare back at him, her heart going wild, as if he was holding her captive in the palm of his hand.

"And second," he said silkily, "if we had, you wouldn't have to ask. You'd know."

"Oh," Adriana said faintly, not sure she was breathing. "Well. If you're sure…?"

Pato shook his head. "I'm sure."

She believed him. He was only *looking* at her now, all that gleaming attention of his focused on her. He wasn't even touching her, and she felt branded. Scalded. Changed. She had a perfect memory of his hand on her arm, the heat of it, the punch of it, the way everything inside her had wound deliciously tight. She believed him, and yet there was something inside her that almost wished—

Stop, she snapped at herself, off balance and scared and much too close to falling apart.

Adriana realized belatedly that far too much time had passed and she'd done nothing but stare at him, while he watched her and no doubt read every last thought that crossed her mind. He was lethal; she understood that now, in a way she hadn't before. He was lethal and she was in bed with him and somehow by the grace of God she hadn't succumbed to his darker nature or, worse, *hers...*

Adriana frowned. "Did you say I *begged?*"

Pato smiled.

"For what?" she asked in an appalled whisper. "Exactly?"

He smiled wider.

"This can't be happening." She was barely audible, even to her own ears, but she felt each word like a stone slamming through her. "Did I—" But even as she asked, she shut herself off. "No. I don't want to know."

"You begged very prettily," he told her then, that wild gleam in his eyes, which made her feel much too hot, too constricted, as if she might burst wide-open. "If it helps."

It helped confirm that she hated herself, Adriana thought, that old black wave of self-loathing rising in her and then drenching her, drowning her, in all the ways she'd let herself down. *Blood really will tell,* she thought bitterly. *You've been fooling yourself all these years, but in the end, you're no better than any of them. Righetti whores.*

She managed to take a breath, then another one.

And then, through her confusion, one thing became perfectly clear: it was time to accept who she was, once and for all. And that meant it was time to change her life.

"Thank you, Your Royal Highness," she said stiffly, not looking at him. "I'm sorry that I let myself get so out of control and that you had to deal with me. How incredibly unprofessional."

She scrambled to crawl out of the bed, away from him. This had to end. What was she was doing here, disgracing herself with a prince, when she could be living without the weight of all of this in some happy foreign land like her brothers? She'd been so desperate to prove herself—and now she'd proved only that she was exactly who everyone thought she was.

Enough, she thought grimly.

And there was what Lenz had said, the way he'd said it, but she didn't want to think about that. She didn't want to let it hurt her the way she suspected it would when she did.

It seemed to take an hour to reach the edge of the bed, and as she went to swing her feet to the ground, Pato simply reached out and hauled her back by the arm until she was on her side and facing him. No sheet this time to hide behind. Just far too much of her nearly naked body far too near his. Panic screamed through her, making her skin burst into flames.

"You can't just...*manhandle* people!" she exclaimed heatedly.

Pato shrugged, and the total lack of concern in the gesture reminded her forcefully that, black sheep or not, he was a royal prince. Pampered and indulged. Used to getting whatever he wanted. He wasn't required to concern himself with other people's feelings, particularly hers.

That should have disgusted her. It alarmed her that it didn't.

"I think we're a bit past worrying about professionalism," he said, his voice mild, though his eyes were intent on hers, and his mouth looked dangerous in a new way with his jaw unshaved and his thick hair so unruly.

And all of him *so close.*

"I need to leave," she replied evenly. "The palace, the royal family—I should have done it a long time ago." She started to pull away from him, but he only shifted position and smoothed his hand down to the indentation of her waist. He rested it there, almost idly, and she froze as if he was pressing her to the bed with brute force.

It would have been easier if he had been, she recognized on some level. It would have been unambiguous. But instead he was only touching her, *barely* touching her, and she couldn't seem to form the words to demand he let her go. She only trembled. Inside and out.

And he knew. His eyes gleamed, and he knew.

"At least let me get back under the sheet," she said desperately.

"Why?" He shrugged again, so lazy. So at ease. "You're showing less skin than you would if you were wearing a bikini."

"You've never seen me in a bikini," she managed to say. "It would be inappropriate."

His fingers traced the faintest pattern along the curve of her body, and she could no more help the shiver of goose bumps that rose on her skin than she could turn back time and avoid this scenario in the first place. He looked at the telltale prickle of flesh, his hand tightened at her waist and she let out a tiny, involuntary sound that made his golden gaze darken and focus on her, hot and hungry.

But when he spoke again, his voice was light.

"I hate to be indelicate, Adriana, but I've already seen all of this. You're about eight hours too late for modesty."

"It's time for me to leave," she said, desperate

and determined in equal measure. "You never wanted an assistant in the first place, and I think it's high time I rethink my career prospects."

Pato only raised a dark brow.

"I have no business being at the palace," she said urgently. "The princess was right. If I'd had any idea that working for your brother would harm *his* reputation, I never would have taken the job in the first place. I would never want people to think less of him because of me. I would never want to compromise his reputation, or—"

"You can't possibly be this naive."

Something Adriana had never seen before moved over Pato's face. His hand tightened briefly, and then he released her and sat up in a smooth roll.

He shoved his hair back and pinned her with a glare when she scrambled away from him and to her knees on the far side of the bed, pulling the sheet back over her as she went. She had never seen him look like that. Brooding, dark. No hint of his famous laughter, his notorious smile.

"I'm being rational, not naive," she countered, unable to tear her eyes away from him when he looked like this, as if he was someone else. Someone ruthless and hard. Not like easy, careless Pato at all. "Your brother was the first person to believe in me, but it was wrong of me to take advantage of that."

Pato shook his head, rubbing at his jaw with one hand as if he was keeping words back manually.

"I abused his kindness," she continued, her unease growing. "His—"

"For God's sake, Adriana," Pato spat out. "He wasn't being *kind*. He was grooming you to be his mistress."

CHAPTER FOUR

FOR A LONG, breathless moment, Adriana could only stare at him, another piece of her world crumbling into dust in this bed, shattering in that relentless golden gaze.

"That's absurd." She felt turned inside out. "He would never do something like that."

"You know all about his previous assistants, I'm sure," Pato said, in that same blunt way, a hard gleam in his gaze and no hint of a curve on that mouth of his. "Did you never question why he cycled so many of them through that position? And why they all had such different sets of credentials? One an art historian, another a socialite? Lenz prefers his mistresses be accessible."

Adriana felt as if she'd slipped sideways into some alternate reality, where nothing made sense any longer. Lenz had wanted her, all this time, as she'd so often daydreamed he might—but not as his mistress. She'd never wanted *that*. And now she sat too close to naked in the morning sun with Pato, of all people, who looked like some harsher version of himself, and she was terrified that he might be right. Hadn't her father said the same thing only yesterday?

"He's a good man," she whispered, shaken.

"Yes," Pato said impatiently. "And yet he's still flesh and blood like all the rest of us."

She shook her head, and looked down at the bed. She'd done this. She understood that, if nothing else. This was the Righetti curse. *This was her fault.* Her head felt heavy again, and it pounded, but she knew it wasn't a leftover from last night. It was the generations of Righettis running wild in her blood, and her silly notion she could be any different.

"Do people really think that I'm his mistress?" she asked, sounding like a stranger to her own ears. She was afraid to look at Pato then, but she made herself do it anyway. His eyes seemed darker than usual, and they glittered.

"Of course." There was an edge to his low voice then, a darker sheen to that intent way he looked at her. "You are a Righetti, he is a Kitzinian prince, and one thing we know about history, Adriana, is that it repeats itself until it kills us all."

Suddenly, the fact that she was practically naked with this man seemed obscene, disgusting. As if her flesh itself were evil, as if it had made her do this—her body ignoring her brain and acting of its own accord. She slid out of the bed and looked around wildly, her eyes falling on the nearest chair. She walked over and grabbed the oversize wrap that she'd worn against the cool London weather, dropped the sheet that made everything seem too sexual, and covered herself.

It didn't make her feel any better.

Adriana couldn't understand how she'd been so blind, so stupid. How she hadn't known that *of course* people would think the worst of her, no matter if the tabloids had eased off—out of respect for Lenz, she understood now in a miserable rush of insight. No one had cared that she was good at her job, that she'd never so much as touched the future king. Why had she imagined any of that would matter? *Because you wanted to pretend. Because you wanted to believe you could be someone else.*

But she was a Righetti. There was never any mistaking that. She should have known it would poison everyone and everything she came into contact with. Even Lenz.

She turned then, and Pato still watched her, sitting there on his bed, a vision of indolent male beauty. Every inch of him royal, gorgeous and as utterly, deliberately corrupt as it was assumed she was. He'd chosen it. He was the Playboy Prince, scandalous and dissolute. But he was still a prince.

Adriana blinked. "So are you," she said slowly, as an idea took root inside her, and began to grow. "A Kitzinian prince, I mean."

Pato's mouth crooked. "To my father's everlasting dismay, yes."

It was so simple, Adriana thought then, staring at him as if she'd never seen him before. It could fix everything.

"Then we should make them all think that I'm *your* mistress," she said in a rush. She clutched the wrap tighter around her, drifting closer to the bed as she spoke. "The tabloids are halfway there already."

"I beg your pardon?"

"No one would be at all surprised to discover that *you* were sleeping with a Righetti," she continued excitedly, ignoring the odd, arrested look on his face. "Your brother is much too responsible to make that kind of mistake. But you live for mistakes. You're famous for them!"

"I'm not following you," he said, and she noticed then that his voice had gone low and hot, and not with the kind of heat she'd heard before.

"It wouldn't even take that much effort." She was warming to the topic as her mind raced ahead, picturing it. "One paparazzi picture and the whole world would be happy to believe that history was indeed repeating itself, but with a far more likely candidate than your brother."

Pato only looked at her for a long moment, and Adriana found herself remembering, suddenly, that he was second in line to the throne. One tragedy and he would be king. All of a sudden he looked as commanding, as regal, as a man in such a position should. Powerful beyond measure. Dangerous.

It was as if she hadn't seen him before. As if he'd been hiding, right there in plain sight, beneath the dissipated exterior. But how was that possible?

"It wouldn't be real, of course," she said quickly, confusion making her feel edgy. Or maybe that was him. "All we'd need was a few pictures and some good PR spin."

He laughed then, but it was a low, almost aggressive sound, and it made her whole body stiffen in reaction.

"You can't possibly be suggesting that we pretend you're sleeping with me to preserve my brother's reputation," he said softly, and Adriana didn't miss the fact that the tone he used was deadly. It made her stomach twist. "You are not actually standing here in my bedroom, wearing almost nothing, and proposing such a thing."

She searched his face, but he was a stranger, dark and hard.

"That's exactly what I'm proposing."

His jaw worked. His golden eyes flashed. "No."

She scowled at him. "Why not?"

"Do you really require a reason?" he demanded, and then he got to his feet, making everything that much more tense. "You'd be much better served making certain we both forget this absurd conversation ever happened."

That was when Adriana realized, in a kind of shock, that he was angry. Pato, who famously never got angry. Who was supposed to be carefree and easy in all things. Who had laughed off every sticky situation he'd ever been in.

But not this one. Not today. He was *angry*. And she had no idea why.

She watched him warily as he roamed around the foot of the bed, so close to naked, and now that temper she hadn't known he had spilling out around him like a black cloud. But she couldn't stop. Not when she'd figured out a way to fix things. And what did he care, anyway? It wasn't as if *his* reputation was at stake.

"I don't understand," she said after a moment, trying to sound reasonable. Rational. "You've gone out of your way to link yourself to every woman with a bad reputation you've ever come across. Why not me? My bad reputation goes back centuries!"

"I actually did those things," he replied, that dark temper rich in his voice, in the narrow gaze he aimed at her. "I didn't pretend for the cameras. I don't apologize for who I am, but I also don't fake it."

Adriana blinked. "So your issue isn't the idea itself, then. It's that you need your debaucheries to be honest and truthful. Real."

The way he looked at her then made a low, dark pulse begin to drum in her, panic and heat and something else she'd never experienced before and couldn't name. It took everything she had not to bolt for the door and forget she'd ever started this.

"My reputation is my life's work," Pato said, and there was a certain harshness in his voice then, dark and grim and tired, that made something clutch hard in Adriana's chest. "It's not a cross I'm forced to bear. It's deliberate."

"Fine," she blurted out. She'd never felt so desperate. She only knew this had to happen, she had to have the opportunity to fix one thing her family name had ruined, just one thing—

"Fine?" he echoed, his golden eyes narrowing, focusing in on her in a way that should have made her fall over in a dead faint. Incinerate on the spot. Run.

Something.

But she met his gaze squarely instead.

"We don't have to fake it," Adriana said, very distinctly, so there could be no mistake. "I'll sleep with you."

All the air in the room evaporated into a shimmer of heat. Into the intensity of Pato's gaze, the electricity that arced between them, the tension bright and taut and very nearly painful.

He laughed, low and dark and wicked, and Adriana felt it like a touch, as if his strong, elegant hands were directly on her skin. It made her feel weak. It made her want to drop the wrap and press herself against him, to see if that might ease the heavy ache inside her, the pulse of it, the need.

But who was she kidding? She knew it would. And so did he.

"You have no idea what you're asking, Adriana," he scoffed. His mouth curved mockingly, knowingly, and that ache in her only grew sharper, more insistent. She suddenly wasn't at all sure what she was desperate for. But she couldn't look away. "You wouldn't know where to start."

Adriana couldn't stop the shivering, way down deep inside her.

Her bones felt like jelly and she didn't know what scared her more—that she might really follow through and throw herself at him, and God only knew what would become of her then, or that the terrible ache inside her might take her to the ground on its own, and then he'd know exactly how much he tormented her.

Though she suspected he already did.

Pato was coming toward her, that sun-kissed skin

on careless display, the faint brush of dark hair across his hard pectoral muscles seeming to emphasize his fascinating, unapologetic maleness. And he watched her so intently as he moved, his golden eyes gleaming as if all the wickedness in the world was in him, dark and rich and his to use against her if he chose. All his.

She shouldn't find that at all intriguing. She shouldn't wonder, now that she'd glimpsed a different side of this man, what else he hid behind his disreputable mask.

This is about Lenz, she reminded herself sharply. She refused to think about Pato's claim that her beloved crown prince had wanted her as his mistress all those years she'd believed they'd been working together in harmony. She couldn't let that matter. This was about saving the one thing she could save, the one thing her family name had blackened that she could actually wash clean.

She couldn't save herself, perhaps. But she could save Lenz's reputation.

"Your brother—" she began.

"Rule number five," Pato said smoothly, but with that alarming kick of dark fire beneath. "When attempting to negotiate your way into my bed, don't bring up my brother. Ever."

Adriana felt her pulse beating too hard inside her neck, her wrists. And lower, where it mixed with that ache in her, gave it bite. She forced herself to stand still as Pato roamed toward her. Forced herself to act as if he didn't, in fact, intimidate her—even when he stopped so close to her that she had to tilt her head back to look at him.

He crossed his arms over his chest, his eyes unreadable.

"Are we negotiating?" she asked, her voice so much smaller than it should have been. Telling him too much she shouldn't let him know.

"I don't take trembling virgins to my bed, Adriana," Pato said, with all that gold in his gaze and that curve to his lips, but still, that new hardness beneath. It almost made her miss what he'd said. Then it penetrated, and her body seemed to detonate into a long, red flush of humiliation—but he wasn't finished. "Particularly not trembling, terrified virgins who imagine themselves in love with my brother and view my bed as a sacrificial altar."

"I—" She'd never stammered in her life. She had to order herself to snap her mouth closed, to calm herself. Or at least to breathe. "I'm not terrified." His gaze never wavered, and yet she was sure it was consuming her where she stood. "And, of course, I'm certainly not a *virgin.*"

His dark brows rose. "Convince me."

"How?" she demanded, bright red and humiliated. And trembling, just as he'd accused. He missed nothing. "Not that it would matter if I was or that it's any of your business, let me point out."

"But it is." He was merciless, his hard gaze hot. "You want in my bed? Then I want to know every last detail of your vast sexual experience. Convince me, Adriana. Consider it a job interview—your résumé. After all, you've read all about me in the tabloids. You said so yourself."

She told herself he couldn't possibly be asking that. *This couldn't possibly be happening.* But then, what part of this day so far was at all possible? She didn't drink to excess and wake up in men's beds. She didn't have extended conversations with royal Kitzinian princes in her underwear. And had she really told this man she would sleep with him?

So she took a deep breath and she told him what she thought he wanted to hear.

"I couldn't possibly count them all," she said

primly, lifting her chin. "I stopped keeping track when I passed into triple digits."

He only shook his head at her.

"For all I know you and I have already slept together, in fact," she continued wildly. "Didn't you once tell an interviewer that you blacked out the better part of the last decade? Well, you're not alone. Who knows where I've been? You were probably there, too, making a spectacle of yourself."

"And somehow," Pato said mildly, "I remain unconvinced."

"Everybody knows I'm a whore," Adriana forced herself to say, not wanting to admit how limited her sexual experience really was. She wasn't a virgin, true—but that was more or less a technicality, and deeply embarrassing to boot. "They've been calling me that since I was a child, before I even knew what the word meant. Why shouldn't I embrace it? You do."

"That doesn't answer the question, does it?" His gaze bored into her, not relenting at all. Not even the smallest bit. "You have not had sexual partners numbering in the triple digits, Adriana. I'd be very much surprised if you've had three in the whole of your life."

And then he simply stood there, staring down at her, somehow knowing these things that he shouldn't. It made her feel almost itchy, as if her skin had stopped fitting her properly. As if she was seconds away from exploding, humiliated and laid unacceptably bare.

"One." She bit out the admission, hating him, hating herself. And yet still as determined to go through with this as she was filled with that terrible, gnawing ache that she worried might consume her alive. *Do it for Lenz,* she ordered herself. "There was only one and it—"

He waited, his eyes intent and demanding on hers, and she couldn't do it. She couldn't tell this sleek, sensual, unapologetically carnal creature about that fumble in the dark, the shock of searing pain and then the unpleasant fullness that followed. That vulnerable, exposed feeling. She'd been seventeen. It had taken all of three unremarkable minutes in a bedroom at a party she shouldn't have gone to in the first place, and then he'd bragged to the whole school that the Righetti girl was as much of a whore as suspected.

"And?" Pato prompted her.

"It was mercifully brief."

"I feel seduced already," he said drily. "What a tempting picture you paint. How can I possibly resist the sacrificial near-virgin who wishes to prostrate herself in my bed for my brother's benefit? I've never been so aroused."

Each dry, sardonic word, delivered in that deliberately stinging way of his, made Adriana's fists tighten where she held the wrap around her. She felt that flush of heat that told her she was getting redder, broadcasting the fact he was getting to her. She felt that twist in her gut and still, that ache below. This was a disaster.

But you have to do it. You'll never be able to live with yourself if you don't. This might be the only opportunity you ever have to do something good with all this notoriety...

"Then teach me," she exclaimed, cutting him off before he could continue ripping her to shreds one sardonic word at a time.

For a moment, Pato only looked at her.

And then he closed the distance between them, reaching out to spear his hands into the wild tangle of her hair, making her go up slightly on her toes and brace her hands against the hot, hard planes of his chest or fall completely against him. Her wrap floated to the floor between them, and she forgot it as he held her face still, keeping her captive, a mere breath away from his beautiful mouth.

She heard a sharp, high sound, some kind of gasp, and realized only belatedly that she'd made it. The echo of it made her tremble, or perhaps that was the wildfire in his eyes.

"Teach me everything," she whispered, spurred on by some dark thing inside her she hardly recognized. But she saw the way his eyes flared, and the ache inside her bloomed in immediate response.

His mouth was so close to hers, his face dark and dangerous, that lethal fire in his gaze. And yet he only held her there, taut and breathless, while sensation after sensation shook through her. Towering flames in her throat, her breasts, her belly. That shocking brightness between her legs.

Her lips parted slightly, and she recognized it as the invitation it was. His gaze dropped to her mouth, hungry and hard, and she felt her nipples pull tight. Nothing existed but that pulse of heat that drummed in her, louder and wilder—

And then he dragged his gaze back to hers and let her go.

She caught herself before she staggered backward, but she was shaky, unbalanced, and for some reason felt as if she might burst into tears. She couldn't seem to form the words she needed, and his eyes darkened because, of course, he knew that, too. He'd done this to her deliberately.

"You can't handle me, Adriana," Pato growled. "Look at you. I've barely touched you and you're coming apart."

That dark thing inside of her roared through her, making her bold. Making her stark, raving mad. But she couldn't hold it in check. She couldn't stop.

She didn't *want* to stop, and she didn't want to think about why.

"It looks like you're the one who's coming apart, Your Royal Highness," she hissed. Taunting him. Poking at him, and she knew it. She wanted it— she wanted *him*—and the obvious truth of that was like another explosion, bathing her in a white-hot heat. Adriana had no choice then but to keep talking despite the way he looked at her. "Maybe your reputation is all lies and misdirection. Maybe the truth is *you* can't handle *me*."

When he laughed then, it was darker than what was inside her, darker and far wilder, and it connected to that ache in her, hard. So hard she stopped breathing.

And then he moved.

His arms came around her and his hands slid over her bottom with an easy command, as if he'd touched her a thousand times before and just as carnally, slipping directly into her panties and pausing to test her curves, her flesh, against the heat of his palms. She made a wild sort of sound, but as she did he hauled her to him and lifted her against him, pulling her legs around his waist even as her back hit the wall behind her.

The room seemed to spin around, but that was only Pato, pressing her to the wall of his chest and the wall at her back, molding his hips to hers, the hardest part of him flush against her. Skin. Heat. Fires within fires, and she was afraid she was already burned to a crisp. Everything hurt—but was eased by the heat of him, only to hurt again. And again.

She expected an explosion. A detonation. Something to match that searing blaze in his gaze, the drum of anticipation beneath her skin, that hunger between her legs that he was only making worse. Her eyes were glazed and wide, and she could feel him everywhere. That perfect, lean body pressed against her, into her, so powerful and male, holding her steady so far from the ground.

His hands moved over her skin, leaving trails of fire in his wake. He traced the curve of her breasts, teased the hard tips with his thumbs until she moaned. He moved his hips, rocking against her, making her breath come in desperate pants even as her core ignited into a glorious, molten ache that she never wanted to end, that she wasn't sure she'd survive.

Adriana couldn't think. She could only hold on to his broad, hard shoulders and surrender to the dark exultation that roared in her, that made her try to get closer to him, that made her think she might die if she couldn't taste him. That made her want things she'd only read about before. That made her want everything.

He leaned in close, so close that when his wicked mouth curved again, she felt it against her own lips, and it made her shake against him, the small moan escaping her before she could stop it.

"Let me see if I can handle this," he mocked her.

"I don't think you can," she heard herself say. "Or you already would have."

As if she was as wanton as he was, and as unashamed. As if she knew what she was demanding.

That smile of his deepened, torturing her. Delighting her.

And then, slowly and deliberately, with one hand on her bottom to move her against him in a sinuous rhythm that made her feel weak, the other at her jaw to hold her where he wanted her, Pato took his own sweet time and licked his way into her mouth.

Ruining her, Adriana thought while the world disappeared, forever.

He never should have tasted her.

That it was a terrible mistake was a certainty, but Adriana clung to him like honey, melting and hot, tasting like sugar and fire with her lithe body wrapped all around him. Pato couldn't stop himself. For a heady moment—his mouth angled over hers, tasting her again and again and again—he even forgot why he should.

This was supposed to be a lesson to her. A way to decidedly call her bluff, nothing more.

And yet he wanted to take her where they stood,

pressed up against the wall, thrusting into the heat of her he could feel scalding him through the thin layers that barely separated them. She was so soft. So responsive.

Perfect.

But she didn't want *him,* no matter what her body shouted at him. No matter what he felt in his arms, what he tasted.

She met him even as he grew bolder, hotter, more demanding. She kissed him as if she'd forgotten who it was she truly wanted. She bloomed beneath his hands, incandescent and addicting. She twined her arms around his neck and writhed against him as if she was as desperate as he was, as if she wanted nothing more than Pato deep inside of her.

But she wanted Lenz. She was in love with Lenz. Pato had seen it.

It was that unpalatable fact that he couldn't make himself ignore, no matter how hard he was and no matter what he would have given, in that moment, to simply drive into her and ride them both into an oblivion where Lenz did not exist. Could never exist.

Where there was only this heat. This need. This delicious electricity, intense and greedy, that made him want to taste every part of her, make her scream out in pleasure while he did, and then take her until she sobbed his name.

His name, not his brother's.

But he couldn't stop. He didn't *want* to stop. What was this woman doing to him? He'd never acted with so little thought before. He'd never forgot to hide himself. He'd certainly never opened his mouth and let some part of the truth come out. It was as if he'd lost the control that had defined him since he was eighteen....

That couldn't happen. He couldn't let it.

He spun around, walking them back to the bed with Adriana still wrapped around him, and then he tortured himself by bringing them down on the mattress—catching himself on one arm so he didn't crush her, but letting himself revel in the feel of her beneath him the way he wanted her, even for a moment.

Pato had never put much stock in the kingdom's insistence that Righetti women were akin to witches, temptresses and jezebels without equal, but pulling himself away from Adriana, from all that soft, hot fire, was the hardest thing he could remember doing.

He didn't understand this. He didn't understand himself.

"I can handle it, Adriana," he told her. "I can handle you. But I won't."

He stood over her, telling himself it didn't matter that she sprawled there before him, her lips swollen from his, her breasts spilling from her bra and crying out for his hands, her silken limbs spread out before him like a dessert he hungered for as if he was a starving man. It didn't matter because it couldn't.

He smirked, knowing it would hit her like a slap. "But I appreciate the offer."

Her face blazed red as he'd thought it would, and she looked tense and unhappy as she pushed herself up to a sitting position. Her lovely blond hair fell in a sexy tangle around her pretty face, making her look as if he'd already had her. He wished he had, with an edge of desperation that should have alarmed him. But she sat before him, with all that lust and wild need still stamped on her face, and the only thing he felt was that pounding desire.

She inclined her head at the clear evidence that he wanted her, badly and unmistakably, then looked up to hold his gaze with hers, her chocolate eyes dark and still too hot.

"I can see how much you appreciate it, Your Royal Highness," she said softly, but with that kick beneath that he couldn't help but enjoy. He didn't understand why he liked her edginess. Why he liked how unafraid she was of him, even now.

He could still taste her. He was so hard for her it hurt, and he wasn't used to denying himself anything. Much less women. He couldn't remember the last time he'd tried. Pato had slept with any number of women who had assumed he'd be a conduit to his brother, who had cold-bloodedly used him for that purpose. It had never bothered Pato before.

He didn't know why it bothered him now—why that look on her face in the shadows last night kept flashing in his head. He only knew he wouldn't—couldn't—be this woman's path to his brother, no matter her reasons, no matter how convoluted it all was. He wanted her head to be full of him, and nothing else.

"We can't always have what we want," he said quietly. He meant it more than she knew.

"You can. You do." She frowned at him. "You've made a career out of it."

Pato shook his head. "You're not going to win this argument with me. No matter how sweetly you pout, or how naked you get. Not that I don't enjoy both."

She made a small sound of frustration, mixed, he could tell from the color in her cheeks, with that embarrassment that he found himself entirely too obsessed with. When was the last time he'd met a woman who still blushed?

"Is there any woman alive you *haven't* slept with?" she demanded. "Or is it only me?"

"It's only you," Pato assured her, not knowing why he was doing this. Not understanding what there was to gain from it. Surely it would be better simply to have her. That was the time-honored approach to situations like this. Chemistry never lasted. Sex was white-hot for only a small while, and then it burned itself out. The only thing denial ever did—or so he'd heard—was make the wanting worse.

But he had never wanted someone like this. And having tasted her, he very much doubted that sex would be a cure. More like his doom.

He didn't know where that thought came from, and yet it clawed into him.

"You didn't even know the word *no* until today!" she snapped at him.

"If I were you," he said in a low voice that he could see got to her when she shivered again, as if he'd run his fingers down the line of her elegant neck, "I'd quit now, before tempers are lost and consequences become far greater. I'd put on some clothes and remember myself. My place. Just a suggestion."

She pulled in a breath, and her hands balled into fists, and then she shook her head slightly as if she really was remembering herself.

"I told you I'd resign," she said after a moment. Her mouth firmed. "And I will. Today, in fact."

"No, you will not."

She *should* resign. He should see to it she was sacked, barred from the palace, kept away for her own good. She should take her melting brown eyes and that impossibly tempting body of hers, her irritating martyr's love for the undeserving Lenz, and leave Kitzinia far behind. She should protect herself from her family's history, from the endless, vicious rumor mill that comprised the highest levels of Kitzinian society, and was even nastier than usual when it came to her.

He wished he could protect her himself.

He was, Pato realized then, in terrible trouble. But this was a game, he reminded himself, and Adriana was a part of it. His strange, protective urges didn't matter—they couldn't. She wasn't going anywhere. He needed her to stay right where she was.

"You won't help me help your brother, and you won't let me leave," Adriana said, her voice as stiff as her body had become, her brown eyes rapidly cooling, which he told himself was better. "What *will* you let me do?"

"I suggest you do your job." It came out harsher than he'd intended, and he saw her blink, as if it hurt. He tried to force his usual laughter into his voice, that devil-may-care attitude he'd perfected, but he couldn't quite do it. "If you can. I can't promise I'll cooperate, but then, you knew that going in."

"I don't want—"

"I am Prince Patricio of Kitzinia and you are a Kitzinian subject," he said, more himself in that moment than he'd allowed himself to be in years, and that, too, was trouble. Big trouble. It was too soon to be anything but Pato the Playboy, even here—and still, he couldn't stop. "You serve at my pleasure, Adriana. Yours is irrelevant."

For a breath, she seemed to freeze there before him. Then she averted her eyes in appropriate deference to his rank, and there was no particular triumph in winning that little skirmish, Pato found. Not when it made him feel empty. Adriana shot to her feet then and started for the door, her spine straight and every inch of her obviously, silently, furious. It hummed in the air between them. He knew it should offend his royal dignity, had he been possessed of any, but it only made him want to taste her again. Taste her temper. Let it take them both on a ride.

"Thank you, Your Royal Highness, for reminding me of my duty. And my place. I won't forget it again."

She spoke as she moved, her words perfectly polite if not *quite* as respectful as they should have been. There was that edge beneath it, that slap, that was all Adriana. It made him hunger for her all over again.

He reached out and snagged her elbow as she

passed, pulling her against him, her back to his front, cursing himself as he did it but completely unable to stop.

"I won't forget this," he said, directly into her ear, all of her soft skin smooth and warm and delicious against his chest, his aching sex. "As you march around to my brother's tune and make your doomed attempts to keep me in line, I'll remember all of this." He let his gaze drift down over her body, satisfaction moving hard in him when her nipples hardened, when another flush worked over her sensitive skin, when her eyes eased closed and her breath went shallow. "I'll remember those freckles between your breasts, for example, three in a line. I'll wonder how they taste. I'll be thinking about the way you look right now, kissed and wild and desperate, when you're ordering me around in your conservative little business suits. It will always be there, hanging in the air between us like a fog."

She shook her head in confusion, and he could feel the fine, delicate tremors that shook in her, the staccato beat of her pulse, all that need and fire and loss. It raged just as brightly in him.

"Then why...?"

Pato leaned closer, spurred on by demons he didn't recognize, needs he didn't understand at all. But their teeth were in him. Deep. And he wanted them in her, too.

"*My* pleasure, Adriana," he told her fiercely, as if it was some kind of promise. A dark threat. He couldn't tell the difference any longer. "Not yours."

CHAPTER FIVE

ADRIANA EYED PATO across the aisle of his royal jet as it winged its way into the night from the glittering shores of Monaco back to Kitzinia, cutting inward across the top of Italy toward Switzerland, Liechtenstein and home.

He was still wearing the formal black tie he'd worn to debonair effect earlier this evening, causing the usual deafening screams when he'd walked the red carpet into the star-studded charity event. Now he murmured into his mobile phone while he lounged on the leather sofa that stretched along one side of the luxury aircraft's lounge area. It had been a long night for him, she thought without a shred of sympathy, as he'd not only had to say a few words at the banquet dinner, but had fended off, at last count, three Hollywood actresses, the lusty wife of a French politician, a determined countess, two socialites and one extremely over-confident caterer.

Left to his own devices, Adriana was well aware, Pato would have stayed in Monaco through the night as he had in years past, partying much too hard with all the celebrities who had flocked to the grand charity event there, and running the risk of either appearing drunk at his engagement with the Kitzinian Red Cross the following morning, or missing it entirely.

She'd insisted they leave tonight. He'd eventually acquiesced.

But Adriana didn't kid herself. She didn't know why he'd pretended to listen to her more often than not in the weeks since that humiliating morning in his London flat. She only knew she found it suspicious.

And that certainly wasn't to suggest he'd *behaved.*

"Your schedule is full this week," she'd told him one morning not long after they'd returned from London, standing stiffly in his office in the palace. Wearing nothing but a pair of battered jeans, he'd been kicked back in the huge, red leather chair behind his massive desk, with his feet propped up on the glossy surface, looking more like a male model than a royal prince.

"I'm bored to tears already," he'd said, his hands stacked behind his head and his golden gaze trained on her in a way that made her want to squirm. She'd somehow managed to refrain. "I think I'd prefer to spend the week in the Maldives."

"Because you require a holiday, no doubt, after all of your hard work doing…what, exactly?"

Pato's mouth had curved, and he'd stretched back even farther in his chair, making his magnificent chest move in ways that only called attention to all those lean, fine muscles packed beneath his sun-kissed skin.

Adriana had kept her eyes trained on his face. Barely.

"Oh, I work hard," he'd told her in that soft, suggestive way that she'd wished she found disgusting. But since London, she'd been unable to dampen the fires he'd lit inside her, and she'd felt the burn of it then. Bright and hot.

"Perhaps if you dressed appropriately," she'd said briskly, forcing a calm smile she didn't feel, and telling herself there was no fire, nothing to burn but her shameful folly, "you might find you had more appropriate feelings about your actual duties, as well."

He'd grinned. "Are my clothes what make me, then?" he'd asked silkily. "Because I feel confident I'm never more myself than when I'm wearing nothing at all. Don't you think?"

Adriana hadn't wanted to touch that, and so she'd listed off his week's worth of engagements while his eyes laughed at her. Charities and foundations. Various events to support and promote Kitzinian commerce and businesses. Tours of war memorials on the anniversary of one of the kingdom's most famous battles from the Great War. A visit to a city in the southern part of the country that had been devastated by a recent fire. Balls, dinners, speeches. The usual.

"Not one of those things sounds like any fun at all," Pato had said, still lounging there lazily, as if he'd already mentally excused himself to the Maldives.

Adriana didn't understand what had happened to her—what she'd done. She shouldn't have responded to him like that in London. She shouldn't have lost her head, surrendered herself to him so easily. So completely. If he hadn't stopped, she knew with a deep sense of shame, she wouldn't have.

And every day she had to stand there before him, both of them perfectly aware of that fact.

It made her hate him all the more. Almost as much as she hated herself. She'd worked closely with Lenz for three years. They'd traveled all over the world together. She'd adored him, admired him. And not once had she so much as brushed his hand inappropriately. Never had she worried that she couldn't control herself.

But Pato had touched her and it had been like cracking open a Pandora's box. Need, dark and wild. Lust and *want* and that fire she'd never felt before in all her life. Proof, at last, that she was a Righetti in more than simply name.

It had to be that tainted blood in her that had made her act so out of character she'd assured herself every day since London. It had to be that infamous Righetti nature taking hold of her, just as the entire kingdom had predicted since her birth, and just as the tabloids claimed daily, speculating madly about her relationship with Pato.

Because it couldn't be him. It couldn't be.

"Yours is a life of great sacrifice and terrible, terrible burdens, Your Royal Highness," she'd said then, without bothering to hide her sarcastic tone.

Forgetting herself the way she did too often around him. "However do you cope?"

For a moment their eyes had locked across the wide expanse of his desk, and the look in his—a quiet, supremely male satisfaction she didn't understand at all, though it made something in her shiver—caused her heart to pound. Erratic and hard.

"Does your lingerie match today, Adriana?" he'd asked softly. Deliberately. Taunting her with the memory of that London morning. "I liked it. Next time, I'll taste it before I take it off you."

Adriana had flinched, then felt herself flush hot and red. She'd remembered—she'd *felt*—his hands on her, slipping into her panties to mold the curves of her backside to his palms, caressing her breasts through her bra. The heat of her embarrassment had flamed into a different kind of warmth altogether, pooling everywhere he'd touched her in London, and then starting to ache anew. And she'd been certain that she'd turned the very same cranberry color as the lingerie she'd worn then as she'd stood there before him in that office.

Pato, of course, had smiled.

She'd opened her mouth to say something, anything. To blister him with the force of all the anger and humiliation and dark despair that swirled in her. To save herself from the truths she didn't want to face, truths that moved in her like blood, like need, like all the rest of the things she didn't want to accept.

"I told you how I feel about challenges," he'd said before she could speak, dropping his hands from behind his head and shifting in his chair, his gaze intense. "Disrespect me all you like, I don't mind. But you should bear in mind that, first, it will reflect on you should you be foolish enough to do it in public, not on me. And second, you won't like the way I retaliate. Do you understand me?"

She'd understood him all too well. Adriana had fled his office as if he'd been chasing her, when all that had actually followed her out into the gleaming hall was the sound of his laughter.

And her own deep and abiding shame at her weakness. But then, she carried that with her wherever she went.

Adriana shifted in her seat now, flipping the pages in her book as if she was reading fiercely and quickly, when in fact she hadn't been able to make sense of a single word since the plane had left the airport in Nice, France. Pato was still on his mobile phone, speaking in Italian to one of his vast collection of equally disreputable friends, his low voice and wicked laughter curling through her, into her, despite her best efforts to simply ignore him.

But she couldn't seem to do it.

Her body remembered London too well, even all these weeks later. It thrilled to the memories. They were *right there* beneath her skin, dancing in her veins, pulsing hot and wild in her core. All it took was his voice, a dark look, that smile, and her body thundered for more. More heat, more flame. More of that darkly addictive kiss. More of Pato, God help her. Adriana was terribly afraid that he'd flipped some kind of switch in her and ruined her forever.

And that wasn't the only thing he'd ruined.

"You are clearly a miracle worker," Lenz had said as the young royals had stood together outside a ballroom in the capital city one evening with their various attendants, waiting to make their formal entrance into a foundation's gala event. "There hasn't been a single scandal since you took Pato in hand."

Adriana had wanted nothing more than to bask

in his praise. Lenz had always been, if not precisely comfortable to be around, at least easy to work for. He'd never been as dangerously beautiful as Pato, but Adriana had always found him attractive in his own, far less flashy way. The sandy hair, the kind blue eyes. He was shorter than his brother, more solid than lean, but he'd looked every inch the king he'd become. It was the way he held himself, the way he spoke. It was who he was, and Adriana had always adored him for it.

Ordinarily, she would have hung on his every word and only allowed herself to think about the way it made her ache for him when she was alone. But that night she'd been much too aware of Pato standing on the other side of the great doorway, with Princess Lissette. Adriana had been too conscious of that golden gaze of his, mocking her. Reminding her.

He was grooming you to be his mistress.

And when she'd looked at Lenz—*really* looked at him, searching for the *man* and not the Crown Prince of Kitzinia she'd always been so awed by— she'd seen an awareness in his gaze, something darker and richer and clearly not platonic.

There had been no mistaking it. No unseeing it. And no denying it.

"I'm afraid I can't take credit for it, Your Royal Highness," she'd said, feeling sick to her stomach. Deeply ashamed of herself and of him, too, though she hadn't wanted to admit that. She'd been so sure Lenz was different. She'd been so *certain*. She hadn't been able to meet his eyes again. "He's been nothing but cooperative."

"Pato? Cooperative? You must be speaking of a different brother."

Lenz had laughed and Adriana had smiled automatically. But she'd been unable to ignore how close he stood to her, how familiar he was when he spoke to her. Too close. Too familiar. Just as her father had warned, and she'd been too blind to see it. Blind and ignorant, and it made her feel sicker.

Worse, she'd been grimly certain that Pato could see every single thought that crossed her mind. And the Princess Lissette had been watching her as well, her cool gaze sharp, her icy words from the ball in London ringing in Adriana's head.

She is widely regarded as something of a pariah.

Adriana had been relieved when it had been time for the royal entrance. They'd all swept inside to the usual fanfare, the other attendants had disappeared to find their own seats and she'd been left behind in the hall, finally alone. Finally away from all those censorious, amused, *aware* eyes on her. Away from Lenz, who wasn't at all who she'd imagined him to be. Away from Pato, who was far more than she could handle, just as he'd warned her.

Adriana had stood there for a very long time, holding on to the wall as if letting go of it might tip her off the side of the earth and away into nothing.

"You seemed so uncomfortable with my brother last night," Pato had taunted her the very next day, his golden gaze hard on her. She'd been trapped in the back of a car with him en route to another event, and she'd felt too raw, too broken, to contend with the man she'd glimpsed in London, so relentless and powerful. She'd decided she preferred him shiftless and lazy, hip deep in scandal. It was easier. "Or perhaps it's only that I expected to see more chemistry between you, given that you wish to make such a great and noble sacrifice to save him."

His tone had been so dry. He was talking about *her life* as if he hadn't punched huge holes right through the center of it. Adriana had learned long ago how to act tough even if she wasn't, how to shrug off the cruel things people said and did to her—but it had been too much that day.

He'd taken everything that had ever meant something to her. Her belief in Lenz. Her position in the palace. Her self-respect. *Everything.* And finally, something had simply cracked.

"I understand this is all a joke to you," she'd said in a low voice, staring out the window at the red-roofed city, historic houses and church spires, the wide blue lake in the distance, the Alps towering over everything. "And why shouldn't it be? It doesn't matter what you do—the people adore you. There are never any consequences. You never have to pay a price. You have the option to slide through life as pampered and as shallow as you please."

"Yes," he'd replied, sounding lazy as usual, but when she'd glanced back at him his gaze was dark. She might have thought he looked troubled, had he been someone else. Her stomach had twisted into a hard knot. "I'm a terrible disappointment. Sometimes even to myself."

Adriana hadn't understood the tension that had flared between them then, the odd edginess that had filled the interior of the car, fragile and heavy at once. She hadn't *wanted* to understand it. But she'd been afraid she did. That Pandora's box might have been opened, and there wasn't a thing she could do to change it after the fact. But that didn't mean that she needed to rummage around inside it, picking up things best left where they were.

"Your brother was the first man who was ever kind to me," she'd said, her voice sounding oddly soft in the confines of the car. "It changed everything. It made me believe—" But she hadn't been able to say it, not to Pato, who couldn't possibly have understood what it had meant to her to feel safe, at last. Who would mock her, she'd been sure. "I would have been perfectly happy to keep on believing that. You didn't have to tell me otherwise."

"Adriana." He'd said her name like a caress, a note she'd never heard before in his voice, and she'd held up a hand to stop him from saying anything further. There had been tears pricking at the back of her eyes and it had already been far too painful.

He would take everything. She knew he would. She'd always known, and it was that, she'd acknowledged then, that scared her most of all.

"You did it deliberately," she'd said quietly, and she'd forced herself to look at him. "Because you could. Because you thought it was *funny*."

"Did you imagine he would love you back?" Pato had asked, an oddly gruff note in his voice then, his gleaming eyes unreadable, and it had hurt her almost more than she could bear. "Walk away from his betrothal, risk the throne he's prepared for all his life? Just as the Duke of Reinsmark did for your great-aunt Sandrine?"

"It wasn't about what Lenz would or wouldn't do," she'd whispered fiercely, fighting back the wild tilt and spin of her emotions, while Pato's words had dripped into her like poison, bitter and painful. "People protect those they care about. If you cared about anything in the world besides pleasuring yourself, you'd know that, and you wouldn't careen through your life destroy—"

He had reached over and silenced her with his finger on her lips, and she hadn't had time to analyze the way her heart slammed into her ribs, the way her whole body seemed to twist into a dark, sheer ripple of joy at even so small and furious a touch from him.

"Don't."

It had been a command, a low whisper, his voice a rough velvet, and that had hurt, too. The car had come to a stop, but Pato hadn't moved. He hadn't looked away from her, pinning her to her seat with too much darkness in his gaze and an expression she'd never seen before on his face, making him a different man all over again.

"You don't know what I care about," he'd told her in that low rasp. "And I never thought any of that was *funny.*"

She'd felt that touch on her mouth for days.

"Ci vediamo," Pato said into his mobile with a laugh now, ending his call.

Adriana snapped back into the present to find him looking at her from where he lounged there across the plane's small aisle. She felt as deeply disconcerted as if the scene in the car had only just happened, as if it hadn't been days ago, and she was afraid he could take one look at her and know exactly what she was thinking. He'd done it before.

If he could, tonight he chose to keep that to himself.

"Good book?" he asked mildly, as if he cared.

"It's enthralling," she replied at once. "I can't bear to put it down for even a second."

"You haven't looked at it in at least five minutes."

"I doubt you were paying that much attention," she said coolly. "Certainly not while making juvenile plans to wreak havoc across Italy with your highly questionable race car driving friends who, last I checked the gossip columns, think the modeling industry exists purely to supply them with arm candy."

He laughed as if she delighted him, and she felt it everywhere, like the touch of the sun. He moved in her like light, she thought in despair, even when he wasn't touching her. She was lost. If she was honest, she'd been lost from the start, when he'd stood there before her with such unapologetic arrogance, naked beneath a bedsheet, and laughed at the idea that she could make him behave.

She should have listened to him. She certainly shouldn't have listened to Lenz, whose motivations for sending her to Pato in the first place, she'd realized at some point while standing in that hallway after seeing him again, couldn't possibly be what she'd imagined them to be when she'd raced off to do his bidding. And she couldn't listen to the tumult inside her, the fire and the need, the chaos that Pato stirred in her without even seeming to try, because that way lay nothing but madness. She was sure of it.

Adriana didn't know what she was going to do.

"Keep looking at me like that," Pato said then, making her realize that she'd been staring at him for far too long—and that he was staring back, his eyes gleaming with a dark fire she recognized, "and I won't be responsible for what happens next."

Pato expected her to throw that back in his face. He expected that cutting tongue of hers, the sweet slap of that smile she used like a razor and sharpened so often and so comprehensively on his skin. He liked both far more than he should.

But her eyes only darkened as they clung to his, and a hectic flush spread over those elegant cheekbones he wanted to taste. He was uncomfortably hard within the next breath, the wild, encompassing need he'd been trying to tell himself he'd imagined, or embellished, slamming into him again, sinking its claws deep, making him burn hot, and *want*.

How could he want her this much?

It had been weeks since London, and his fascination with her should have ebbed by now, as his little fascinations usually did in much less time. And most of *those* women had not fancied themselves tragically in love with his brother. But Adriana was always with him, always right there within his reach, prickly and unimpressed and severe. He spent his days studying her lovely face and its many masks, reading her every gesture, poking at her himself when he grew tired of the distance she tried to put between them.

This woman was his doom. He understood that on a primal level, and yet couldn't do the very thing he needed to do to avert it. He couldn't let her walk away. That was part of the game—but he found he couldn't bear the thought of it.

And he didn't like to think about the implications of that.

"Careful, Adriana," he said quietly. Her chest rose and fell too fast and her hands clenched almost fitfully at the thick paperback she held. If he asked, she would claim she didn't want him and never had—but he could see the truth written all over her. He recognized what burned in her, no matter what she claimed. It made him harder, wilder. Closer to desperate than he'd been in years. "I'm in a dangerous mood tonight."

She blinked then, looking down into her lap and smoothing her hands over the abused book, and he had rendered himself so ridiculous when it came to this woman that he felt it like loss.

"I don't know how you can tell the difference between that and any of your other moods," she said in her usual sharp way, which Pato told himself was better than that lost, hungry stare that could only lead to complications he knew he should avoid. "They're all dangerous, sooner or later, aren't they? And we both know who'll have to clean up the mess."

"I expected applause when we boarded the plane," he told her, smiling when her gaze came back to his, her brows arched over those warm, wary eyes that made him forget about the hollow places inside him. "A grateful speech or two, perhaps even a few thankful tears."

"You board planes all the time," she pointed out, her expression smooth, and that decidedly disrespectful glint in her dark eyes that he enjoyed far too much. "I was unaware that you required encouragement to continue doing so. I'll be sure to make a note of that for future reference. Perhaps the Royal Guard can break from their regular duties protecting our beloved sovereign, and perform a salute."

"I want only your applause, Adriana," he told her silkily. "After all, you're the one who insisted I become chaste and pure, and so I have. At your command."

"I'm sorry," she murmured, something that looked like a smirk flashing across her mouth before she wisely bit it back. "Did you describe yourself as 'chaste and pure'? In an airplane, of all places, where we are that much closer to lightning, should you be struck down where you sit?"

She was a problem. A terrible problem, the ruin of everything he'd worked for all these years, but Pato couldn't seem to keep himself from enjoying her. He couldn't seem to do anything but bask in her. Tart and quick and the most fun he'd had in ages. With that sweet, hot fire beneath that would burn them both.

"Shall I tell you what I got up to at this particular benefit last year?" he asked.

"Unnecessary," she assured him. "The video of your ill-conceived spa adventure is still available on the internet. Never has the phrase 'the royal jewels' been so widely and hideously abused."

He laughed, and spread out his hands in front of him as if in surrender—noting the way her eyes narrowed in suspicion, as if she knew exactly how unlikely it was he might ever truly surrender anything.

"And look at me now," he invited her. "Not a single lascivious actress in sight, no spa tub in a hotel room that was meant to be private, and I'm not even drunk. You should be proud, Adriana."

She shifted in her chair, crossing her legs, and then frowning at him when his gaze drifted to trace the elegant line of them from the hem of her demure skirt down to the delicate heels she wore.

"Your transformation has been astonishing," she said in repressive tones when he grinned back at her. "But you'll forgive me if I can't quite figure out your angle. I only know you must have one."

"I prefer curves to angles, actually," he said, and laughed again at her expression of polite yet clear distaste at the innuendo. "And it has to be said, I've always found lingerie a particularly persuasive argument."

Adriana let out a breath, as if he'd hit her. Something terribly sad moved over her face then, surprising him and piercing into him. She ran her hands down the length of her skirt, smoothing out nonexistent wrinkles, betraying her anxiety.

Pato knew he was a bastard—he'd gone out of his way to make sure he was—but this woman made him feel it. Keenly. She made him wish he was a different man. A better one. The sort of good one she deserved.

"Perhaps you've managed to convince me of the error of my ways," he said quietly, hating himself further because he wasn't that man. He couldn't be that man, no matter how much she made him wish otherwise. "Just because it hasn't been done before doesn't mean it's impossible."

Her dark eyes met his and made something twist in him, sharp and serrated.

"We both know I did nothing of the kind," she said, her voice soft and matter-of-fact. She let out a small breath. "All I managed to do was make myself one among your many conquests, indistinguishable from the rest of the horde."

"I don't know why you'd think yourself indistinguishable," he said, keeping his tone light.

He could have sworn what he saw flash in her dark eyes then was despair, but she swallowed it back and forced a smile that made his chest hurt.

"I should have realized," she said, and he wondered if she knew how bitter she sounded then, how broken. "You've always been a trophy collector, haven't you? And what a prize you won in London. You get to brag that the Righetti whore propositioned you and you—*you,* of all people—turned her down. My congratulations, Your Royal Highness. That's quite a coup."

For a long moment a black temper pulsed in him, and Pato didn't dare speak. He only studied her face. She was pale now, and sat too straight, too stiff. Her eyes were dark again in exactly the same way they'd been that morning in the car, when he'd felt pushed to confront her about Lenz, and was fairly certain she'd broken his heart. Had he had one to break.

Pato hated this. He was perilously close to hating himself. For the first time since he was eighteen, he wished that he could do exactly what he wanted without having to worry about anyone else. Without having to play these deep, endless games. Adriana sat there and looked at him as if he was exactly the depraved degenerate he'd gone to great lengths to ensure he really was, when she was the first woman he'd ever met that he wanted to think better of him. The irony wasn't lost on him.

It stung. *Congratulations, indeed,* he thought ruefully. This was what doom looked like as it happened, and he was doing nothing at all to prevent it.

"Adriana," he said, trying to keep his temper from his voice. Trying to make sense of his determination to protect her not only from the things he shouldn't allow himself to want from her, but from herself. "You and I both know you're no whore. Why do you torture yourself over the lies that strangers tell? They're only stories. They're not even about you."

"On the contrary," she said after a moment, her voice thick and uneven. "Some of us are defined by the stories strangers tell."

"You're the only one who can define yourself," he countered gently. "All they can do is tell another story, and who cares if they do?"

Emotion moved through her then, raw and powerful. He saw it on her face, in the way her eyes went damp, in the faint tremor of her lips. Her hands balled into fists in her lap and she moved restlessly in her seat, stamping both feet into the floor as if she needed the balance.

"Easy for you to say," she stated, a raw edge to her voice. "Not all of us can be as beloved as you are no matter what you do, forgiven our trespasses the moment we make them."

"Fondness is hardly the same thing as forgiveness."

Her dark eyes seared into him. "You cheerfully admit each and every one of your transgressions," she said. "There are videos, photographs, whole tabloids devoted to your bacchanals. But you are still the most popular young royal in all of Europe. No one cares how dirty you get. It doesn't cling to you. It doesn't matter."

"I prefer 'adventurous' to 'dirty,' I think," he said mildly, watching her closely, seeing nothing but shadows in her beautiful eyes. "Especially in that tone."

"Meanwhile," she said, as if he hadn't spoken, "I happen to be related to three women who slept with Kitzinian royalty over a hundred and fifty years ago, and one woman who ruined a duke more recently. I'm the most notorious slut in the kingdom, thanks to them." She pulled in a breath. "It isn't even *my* dirt, but I'm covered in it, head to toe, and I'll never be clean. Ever." Her eyes held his for a long moment, fierce and dark. "It isn't just another story strangers tell. It's my life."

Pato was aware that he needed to shut this down now, before he forgot himself. But instead, he shook his head and continued talking, as if he was someone else. Someone with the freedom to have dangerous conversations with a woman he found far too fascinating, as if both of them weren't pawns in a game only he knew they were playing.

"You must know that almost all of that is jealousy," he said, letting out a small laugh at the idea that she didn't. "You're a legend, Adriana, whether you earned it or not. Women are envious of the attention you get, simply because you have a notorious name and the temerity to be beautiful. Men simply want you."

She let out a frustrated noise, and snatched up her book again, that smooth mask of hers descending once more. But he could see right through it now.

"I don't want to discuss this," she said, more to the book than to him. "You can't possibly understand. There's not a day of your life you've been envious of anyone, because why should you be? And you certainly don't *want* me. You made that perfectly clear in London."

Pato didn't know he meant to move. He shouldn't have. But one moment he was on the couch and the next he was looming over her, swiveling her chair around and leaning over her, into her, planting his hands on the armrests and caging her between his arms. Risking everything, and he didn't care.

"I never said I didn't want you," he growled down at her.

Pato felt unhinged and unpredictable, capable of anything. Especially a mistake of this magnitude—but he couldn't seem to stop himself. Adriana still smelled of jasmine and her eyes were that rich, deep brown, and he didn't have it in him to fight off this madness any longer.

"Not that I want to revisit the most humiliating morning of my life," she said from between her teeth, "but you did. If not in words, then in actions. And don't misunderstand me, I'm grateful. I wasn't myself."

"The question on the table that morning was not whether or not I wanted you." He moved even closer, watching in satisfaction as her pretty eyes widened with a shock of awareness he felt like hands on his skin. "The question was whether or not I wanted to sleep with you knowing full well you planned to shut your eyes and imagine Lenz in my place. They're not quite the same thing."

She paled, then burst into that bright red blush that Pato found intoxicating. He liked her cheeks rosy, her cool exterior cracked and all her masks useless, the truth of her emotions laid bare before him.

"What does it matter?" Her voice was barely a whisper. "It didn't happen. Crisis averted. There's no need to talk about it now."

"I told you I wouldn't forget," he said, intent and hungry, "and I haven't. I remember the noises you made in the back of your throat when I kissed you, when you rubbed against me like silk, hot and—"

"Please!" Her voice was low. Uncertain. "Stop."

"What do *you* want, Adriana? That's tonight's question."

He leaned in closer, so he could hear the tiny hitch in her breath, and so he could find the pulse in her neck that was drumming madly, giving her away, and tease it with his tongue.

She whispered something that came out more a

moan, and he smiled against the delicate column of her throat. Her skin smelled of his favorite flowers and her hair smelled of holidays in the sun, and he wanted to be deep inside her more than he wanted his next breath.

"And when I talk about *want,* I don't mean something tame," he said, a growl against the side of her neck, directly into her satiny skin, so he could feel her tremble against his lips. "I mean hunger. Undeniable, unquenchable hunger. Not because you're drunk. Not because you want to martyr yourself to your great unrequited love. *Hunger,* Adriana. What do you want? What are you hungry for?"

"Please…" she whispered, desperation thick in her voice. She was right there on the edge, right where he wanted her. He could feel it. He felt it flood through him, dark and thrilling and scorchingly hot.

"I don't think you love him, Adriana," he told her then, and she let out a small sound of distress. "Not really. I know you're not hungry for him. Not like this."

She trembled. She shook. But she didn't argue.

"I asked you a question," he urged her, his mouth at her jaw. "If it helps, I already know the answer. All you have to do is admit it."

CHAPTER SIX

ADRIANA'S BREATH CAME out like a sigh. A release.

Like surrender, Pato thought, satisfaction moving through him like another kind of need, dark and demanding, like all the ways he wanted her.

"I thought it would help your brother's reputation," she said almost too softly, her eyes bright with heat. "I really did."

He nipped at her jaw, and she shivered.

"But I never would have suggested—" She broke off, bit her lip in agitation, then tried again. "I mean, I wouldn't have thought of it if I didn't—"

Pato waited, but she only pulled in a ragged breath, then another. She could hardly sit still. She was flushed hot, shining with the same need he felt pulling at him. Coming apart, right there in the chair, and he'd hardly touched her.

She was going to be the end of him. He knew it. He couldn't wait.

"Say it," he ordered her. "If you didn't…?"

He felt her give in to it before he saw it, a shift in that tension that tightened the air between them. And then her shoulders lowered, she let out a long breath, and what stormed in him then felt like much, much more than simple victory.

"If I didn't want you," she admitted hoarsely.

Pato kissed her, hard and long and deep, his fingers spearing into her sleek chignon and sending pins scattering to the floor.

And she met him, the feel of her mouth beneath his again—at last—like a revelation.

He couldn't get enough of her taste. He angled his jaw for a better fit and it got hotter, wilder, and then he thought he might explode when he felt her hands running along his arms, trailing over his chest, making him wish he could remove all the layers of his formal clothes simply by wishing them away.

He wanted her mindless. Now. He wanted her falling apart in his arms, lost to this passion that might very well destroy them both. He wanted to claim her.

Pato broke away from the glory of her mouth and sank to his knees before her, making room for himself between her legs. She made a small, dazed sort of sound. He grinned at her, then simply pulled her hips toward him, pushing her skirt up toward her waist and out of his way as he positioned her at the edge of her seat.

He ran his palms up her smooth, satiny thighs, grinning wider as she bit back a moan. He sank his hands underneath her, grasping her perfect bottom and ducking lower, arranging her so that her legs fell over his shoulders and hung down his back. Then he tilted her hips toward him.

"Oh, my God," she whispered, slumped down in her chair with her skirt around her waist and that delectable flush heating her face, making her dark chocolate eyes melt and shine as they met his.

She was delicious and shivering and his. All his, at last.

God help them both.

"Hold on," Pato advised her, hardly recognizing his own voice, so stark with desire was it. So focused. "You'll need it."

He lifted her to him, smiling at the pretty scrap of blue lace that covered the sweet heat of her, and then he leaned forward to suck her into his mouth.

The shock of his mouth against the very center of her need took Adriana's breath, so that the scream she let out sounded only inside her, ricocheting like a bullet against glass and shattering whatever it touched.

The heat. The fire. The terrible, wonderful ache.

His wicked, talented mouth, so hot and demanding, pressed against the tiny layer of lace that separated them. His hard shoulders felt massive and the fabric of his jacket rough against the tender skin behind her knees. His clever hands gripped her and held her fast, and his impossibly beautiful face was between her thighs so that all she could see when she looked down was that thick, wild hair of his, sunshine and chocolate and that delicious bit too long, and her own hands fisted in the mass of it as if they'd gone there of their own accord.

She thought she'd died. She wanted to die. She didn't know how anyone could take this much pleasure, this much scalding heat, and live through it—

And then he made a low noise of male pleasure, shoved her thong out of his way and licked deep into her molten core.

Adriana burst into a firestorm of white-hot heat and exploded over the edge of the world, lost in a shower of shivering flames.

When she was herself again, or whatever was

left of her, she couldn't seem to catch her breath. And Pato was laughing in dark masculine delight, right there against the heat of her core, making the pleasure curl in her all over again, sweeter and hotter than before.

"Again, I think," he murmured, each syllable humming into her and making her press against him before she knew she meant to move, greedy and mindless and adrift in need.

And he took her all over again.

He used his tongue and the scrape of his teeth. His mouth learned her, possessed her, commanding and effortless. His jaw moved against the tender skin of her thighs, the faint rasp of his beard making the fire in her reach higher, burn hotter. The hands that held her to him caressed her, a low roll of sensation that made her shudder and writhe against him, into him, wanting nothing in the world but this. Him.

And that coiling thing inside her that he knew exactly how to wind tight. Then tighter. Then even tighter still.

Adriana felt the fire surge into something almost unbearable, her whole body stretched taut and breathless, heard his growl of approval and her own high, keening noise—

And then, again, she was nothing more than the fire and the need, shattering into a thousand bright, hot pieces against his wicked, wicked mouth, and then falling in flames all around him.

When Adriana opened her eyes this time, reality slammed into her like a hammer at her temples.

What had she done?

Pato had moved to lounge on the floor, his back against the couch opposite her, with his long legs stretched out and nearly tangled with hers. He wasn't smiling. Those golden eyes were trained on her, brooding and dark, and she didn't know how long she stared back at him, too shaken and dazed to do anything else.

But that hammer kept at its relentless pounding, and she forced her gaze from his, looking down at herself as if he'd taken her body from her and re-placed it with someone else's. That was certainly what it felt like.

She thought she might cry. Adriana struggled to sit upright, tugging her skirt back down toward her knees, aware as she did so that she could still feel him. That mouth of his all over the core of her, his hands wrapped so tightly over her bottom. It felt as if every place he'd touched her was a separate drum, and each beat in her with its own dark pulse.

Then something else hit her, and she froze. She didn't have much practical experience, but Adriana recognized that what had happened had been…unequal. She swallowed nervously, sneaked a glance at him and then away.

"You didn't—" She was still in pieces and wasn't sure she'd ever manage to reassemble herself. Not the way she'd been before. Not now that he'd demonstrated exactly how much she'd been lying to herself. She cleared her throat. "I mean, if you'd like…"

"How tempting," Pato said drily when she couldn't finish the sentence, his gaze harder when she met it, a darker shade of gold she'd never seen before. "But I prefer screams of passion to insincere sacrifices, thank you. To say nothing of enthusiastic participants."

And the worst part, she realized, as her heart kicked at her and made her feel dizzy, was that she couldn't run from him the way she had that morning in London. She couldn't find a far-off corner of his luxurious penthouse and hide herself away until she wrestled her reactions under control. They were on a plane. There was no hiding from what she'd done this time. No rationalizations, no excuses. And she hadn't had anything to drink but water all night long.

The silence between them stretched and held, nothing but the sound of the jet's engines humming all around them, and Adriana didn't have the slightest idea what to do. She was aware of him in ways she suspected would haunt her long after this flight was over, ways she should have recognized and avoided weeks ago. Why had she thought she could handle this—handle him? Why had she been so unpardonably arrogant?

He'd been leading her here all along, she understood. And she'd let him, telling herself that what was happening to her wasn't happening at all. Telling herself stories about tainted blood and Pandora's box. Thinking she could fight it with snappy lines and some attitude.

She'd known she was scraped raw by this, by the things that had happened between them. What he'd done and what he'd said. The brutal honesty, the impossible need. But it was her own appalling weakness that shamed her deep into her bones. That made her wonder if she'd ever known herself at all.

"Why did you do that?" she asked, when the silence outside her head and the noise within was too much.

His dark brows edged higher. There was the faintest twitch of that mouth of his, which she now knew so intimately she could still feel the aftershocks.

"I wanted to know how you tasted," he said.

So simple. So matter-of-fact. So Pato.

A helpless kind of misery surged through her, tangled up with that fire he'd set in her that never died out, and she wished she hadn't asked. She kept her eyes on the floor, where his feet were much too close to hers, and wondered how she could find something so innocuous so threatening—and yet so strangely comforting at the same time.

"Was that your first?" he asked, with no particular inflection in his voice. "Or should I say, your first two?"

"My first...?" she echoed, confused.

And then his meaning hit her, humiliation close behind, and she felt the scalding heat of shame climb up her chest and stain her cheeks. She wanted to curl into a ball and disappear, but instead she sat up straight, as if posture alone could erase what had happened. What she'd done. What she'd let him do to her without a single protest, as if she'd been waiting her whole life to play the whore for him.

Weren't you? that voice spat at her, and she flinched.

"I apologize if I was deficient, Your Royal Highness." She threw the words at him, in an agony of embarrassment. "I neglected to sleep with the requisite seven thousand people necessary to match your level of—"

"There was only the one, I know," he interrupted, his even tone at odds with the storm in his eyes and that unusually straight line of his mouth. No crook, no curve. Serious, for once, and it made it all that much worse. "And I imagine all five seconds of unskilled fumbling did not lead to any wild heights of passion on your part."

Adriana couldn't believe this conversation was happening. She couldn't believe any of this had happened. If she could have thrown herself out the plane's window right then and there, she would have. A nice, quiet plummet from a great height into the cold embrace of the Alps sounded like blessed relief.

But Pato was still looking at her. There was no escape.

"Of course it wasn't my first," she managed to say, but she couldn't look at him while she said it. She couldn't believe she was answering such a personal question—but then, he'd had his mouth between her legs. What was the point of pretending she had any boundaries? Any shame? "I might not have cut a swathe across the planet like some, but I didn't take a vow of celibacy."

"With a man," he clarified, and there was the slightest hint of amusement in his eyes then, the faintest spark. "A private grope beneath the covers, just you and your hand in the dark, isn't the same thing at all. Is it?"

Adriana didn't understand how she could have forgotten how much she hated him. She remembered now. It roared through her, battling the treacherous, traitorous embers of that fire he'd licked into a consuming blaze, filling her with the force of it, the cleansing power—

But it burned itself out just as quickly, leaving

behind the emptiness. That great abyss she'd been skirting her whole life, and there was nothing holding her back from it anymore, was there? She had spent three years with Lenz, thinking her dedication proved she wasn't what her surname said she was. And hardly more than a month with Pato, demonstrating exactly why Righetti women were notorious.

She had betrayed herself and her family in every possible way.

And he was still simply looking at her, still sitting there before her as if sprawling on the floor made him less threatening, less diabolical. Less *him.*

Worse, as if he expected an answer.

"Adriana," he began evenly, almost kindly, and she couldn't take it.

She was horrified when tears filled her eyes, that hopelessness washing over her and leaving her cruelly exposed. She shook her head, lifting her hands and then dropping them back into her lap.

He had destroyed her. He'd taken her apart and she'd let him, and she didn't have any idea how she would survive this. She didn't know what to *do.* If she wasn't who she'd always thought she was, if she was instead who she'd always feared she might become, then she had nothing.

Nothing to hold on to anymore. Nothing to fight for. Nothing at all.

"What do you want from me?" she asked him, and she didn't sound like herself, so broken and small. She felt the tears spill over, the heat of them on her cheeks, and she was too far gone to care. Though her eyes blurred, she focused on him, dark and male and still. "Is this it—to make me become everything I hate? Everything I spent my whole life fighting against? Are you happy now?"

He didn't answer, and she couldn't see him any longer, anyway, so she stopped pretending and covered her face with her hands, letting the tears flow unchecked into her palms, her humiliation complete.

She didn't hear him move. But she felt his hands on her, lifting her into the air and then bringing her down on his lap. Holding her, she realized when it finally penetrated. Prince Pato was *holding* her. She tried to push away, but he only pulled her closer, sliding her across his legs so that her face was nestled into the crook of his neck. There was the lightest of touches, as if he'd pressed a kiss to her hair.

He was warm and strong and deliciously solid, and it was so tempting to pretend that they were different people. That this meant something. That he cared.

That she was the kind of woman someone might care for in the first place.

It was shocking how easy it was to tell herself lies, she thought then, despairing of herself—and so very, very sad about how eager she was to believe them. Even now, when she knew better.

"We don't always get to play the versions of ourselves we prefer," Pato said after a long while, when Adriana's tears had faded away, and yet he still held her.

He smoothed a gentle hand over her hair as he spoke, and Adriana found that she didn't have the strength to fight it off the way she should. She couldn't seem to protect herself any longer. Not from him. Not from any of this. She could feel the rumble of his voice in his chest, and had to shut her eyes against the odd flood of emotion that rocked through her.

Too much sensation. Too many wild emotions, too huge and too dangerous. *Too much.*

"I don't think you understand," she whispered.

"The army was the only place I ever felt like a normal person," he replied. Did she imagine that his arms held her closer, more carefully, as if she really was something precious to him? And when had she started wanting him to think so? "None of the men in my unit cared that I was a prince. They cared if I did my job. They treated me the same way they treated each other. It was a revelation." He traced the same path over her hair, making her shiver again. "And if I like Pato the Playboy Prince less than I liked Pato the Soldier, well. One doesn't cancel out the other. They're both me."

There was nothing but his arms around her and the solid heat of him warming her from the inside out. Making her feel as if everything was somehow new. Maybe because he was holding her this way, maybe because he'd told her something about him she hadn't already read in a tabloid. Maybe because she didn't have the slightest idea what to do with his gentleness. Adriana felt hushed, out of time. As if nothing that happened here could hurt her.

It wasn't true, she knew. It never was. But she couldn't seem to keep herself from wanting, much too badly, to believe that just this once, it could be.

"Yes," she said, finding it easier to talk to that strong neck of his, much easier when she couldn't see that challenging golden gaze. She could fool herself into believing she was safe. And that he was. "But none of the versions of you—even the most scandalous and attention-seeking—are called a whore with quite the same amount of venom they use when it's me." He sighed, and she closed her eyes against the smooth, hot skin of his throat. "You know it's true."

She felt him swallow. "What they call you reflects far more on them than on you," he said gruffly.

"Perhaps it did when I wasn't exactly what they called me. But I can't cling to that anymore, can I?"

She pushed herself away from him then, sitting up with her arms braced against his chest so she could search his face, and the way he frowned at her, as if he was truly concerned, made her foolish heart swell.

"You said it yourself," she continued. "Kitzinian

princes and Righetti women. History repeating itself, right here on this plane." His frown deepened and she felt his body tighten beneath her, but she kept going. "I held my head up no matter what they said because I knew they were wrong. But now…" She shrugged, that emptiness yawning inside her again, black and deep. "Blood will tell, you said, and you were right."

Pato's gaze was so intense, meeting hers, that it very nearly hurt.

"What happened between us does not make you a whore."

"I think you'll find that it does. By definition."

His eyes moved over her face, dark and brooding, almost as if she'd insulted him with that simple truth.

"But," he said, his tone almost careful, "you were happy enough to risk that definition when it was your suggestion, and when you thought it would benefit Lenz."

There was no reason that should hurt her. She didn't know why it did. *I don't think you love him,* he'd told her in that low, sure voice.

"That was different," she whispered, shaken.

"That was a plan hatched in desperation. This was…"

She couldn't finish. Pato looked at her for a long moment, and then his eyes warmed again to the gold she knew, his mouth hinted at that wicked curve she'd tasted and felt pressed against her very core, and she didn't know if it was joy or fear that twisted inside her, coiling tight and making it difficult to breathe.

"Passion, Adriana," he said with soft intent. "This was passion."

She told herself she didn't feel that ring inside her like a bell. That there was no *click* of recognition, no sudden swell of understanding. She didn't know what he was talking about, she told herself desperately, but she was quite certain she shouldn't have anything to do with either passion or princes. There was only one place that would lead her, and on this end of history she very much doubted she'd end up with her portrait in the Royal Gallery. Like her great-aunt Sandrine, she'd be no more than a footnote in a history book, quietly despised.

"Passion is nothing but an excuse weak people use to justify their terrible behavior," she told him, frowning.

"You sound like a very grim and humorless cleric," Pato said mildly, his palms smoothing down her back to land at her hips. "Did my mouth feel like a justification to you? Did the way you came apart in my hands feel like an excuse? Or were you more alive in those moments than ever before?"

Adriana pushed at his chest then, desperate to get away from him, and she was all too aware that she was able to climb out of his lap and scramble to her feet at last only because he chose to let her go.

"It doesn't matter what it felt like." She wished her voice didn't still have that telltale rasp. She wished Pato hadn't made it sound as if this was something more than the usual games he played with every female who crossed his path. More than that, she wished there wasn't that part of her that wanted so badly to believe him. "I know what it makes me."

Pato shoved his hair back from his face with one hand and muttered something she was happy she didn't catch. She wanted to make a break for the bathroom and bar herself inside, but her legs were too shaky beneath her, and she sat down on the chair instead, as far away from him as she could get. Which wasn't far at all. Not nearly far enough to recover.

"My mother was a very fragile woman," he said after a long moment, surprising Adriana.

She blinked, not following him. "Your mother?"

Queen Matilda had been an icon before her death from cancer some fifteen years ago. She was still an icon all these years later, beloved the world over. Her grave was still piled high with flowers and trinkets, as mourners continued to make pilgrimages to pay their respects. She had been graceful, regal, feminine and lovely. Her smile had once been called "Kitzinian sunshine" by the rhapsodic British press, while at home she'd been known as the kingdom's greatest weapon.

She had been anything but *fragile*.

"She was so beautiful," Pato said, his voice dark, skating over Adriana's skin and making her wrap her arms around herself. "From the time she was a girl, that was the only thing she knew. How beautiful she was and what that would get her. A king, a throne, adoring subjects. But my father married a pretty face he could add to his collection of lovely things and then ignore, and my mother didn't know what to do when the constant attention she lived for was taken away from her."

Pato's eyes were troubled when they met hers, and Adriana caught her breath. That same celebrated beauty his mother had been so famous for was stamped all over him, though somehow, he made it deeply masculine. He was gilded and perfect, just as she had been before him, and Adriana would never have called him the least bit fragile, either. Until this moment, when he almost looked…

But she couldn't let herself think it. There was too much at stake and she couldn't trust herself. She didn't dare. What he felt wasn't her concern. It couldn't be.

He smiled then, but it wasn't his usual smile. This one felt like nails digging into her, sharp and deep, and she wanted to hold him the way he'd held her, as if she could make him feel safe for a moment, however fleeting.

You're such a fool.

"You don't have to tell me this," she said hurriedly, suddenly afraid of where this was going. What it would do to her if he showed her things she knew he shouldn't. "It's your family's private, personal business."

She wanted him too much. She'd proved it in unmistakable terms, with her legs flung over his shoulders and her body laid open for his touch. Somewhere inside of her, where she was afraid to look because she didn't want to admit it, Adriana knew what that meant. She knew.

He gave half the world his body. She would survive that; his women always did. But if he gave her his secrets, she would never recover.

"So she did the only thing she knew how to do," Pato said, his gaze never leaving Adriana's, once again that different, harder version of himself, every inch of him powerful. Determined. *Bleak,* Adriana thought, and ached for him. "She found the attention she needed."

Adriana stared at him, not wanting to understand what he was saying. Not wanting to make the connection. He nodded, as if he could see the question she didn't want to ask right there on her face.

"There were always men," he said, confirming it, and Adriana hugged herself that much tighter. "They kept her happy. They made her smile, laugh, dance in the palace corridors and pick flowers in the gardens. They made her *herself.* And my father didn't care how many lovers she took as long as she was discreet. He might not have wanted her the way she thought he should, the way she needed to be wanted, but he wanted her happy."

Adriana found it hard to swallow. She could only stare at Pato in shock. And hurt for him in ways she didn't understand. He leaned forward then, keeping his eyes on hers, hard and demanding. She felt that power of his fill the space between them, pressing at her like a command.

"Was my mother a whore, Adriana?" he asked, his voice a quiet lash. "Is that the word you'd use to describe her?"

She felt too hot, then too cold. Paralyzed.

"I can't— You shouldn't—"

Pato only watched her, his mouth in that serious line, and she felt the ruthlessness he hid behind his easy smiles and his laughter pressing into her from all sides and sinking deep into her belly. How had she ever imagined this man was *careless?*

"Of course not," she said at last, feeling outside herself. Desperate. As if what she said would keep her from shaking apart from the inside out. "She was the queen. But that doesn't mean—"

"It's a word people use when they need a weapon," he said, very distinctly, and that look in his eyes made Adriana feel naked. Intensely vulnerable. As if he could see all the ugliness she hid there, the encroaching darkness. "It's a means of control. It's a prison they herd you into because they think you need to be contained."

She shook her head, unable to speak, unable to handle what was happening inside her. Some kind of earthquake, rolling long and hard and destroying foundations she hadn't known she'd built in the first place.

"That's all well and good," she whispered, hardly aware of what she was saying, seeing only Pato and that look on his face, "but there's no one here but you and me and what happened between us, the way I just—"

"Don't do it," he warned her, cutting her off, his eyes flashing. "Don't make it ugly simply because it was intense. There was nothing ugly about it. You taste like a dream and your responsiveness is a gift, not a curse."

What moved in her then was so overwhelming she thought for a long, panicked moment that she might actually be sick, right there on the floor. She was too hot again, then freezing cold, and she might have thought she'd come down with a fever if she hadn't seen the way he looked at her. If she hadn't felt it deep inside her, making so many things she'd taken for granted crumble into dust.

But she couldn't bring herself to look away. She was falling apart—he was making sure she did—and she didn't *want* to look away.

"Don't use their weapons on yourself," he told her then, very distinctly, the royal command and that brooding darkness making her shiver as his gaze devoured her, changed her, demanded she listen to him. "Don't lock yourself in their prison. And don't let me hear you use that word to describe yourself again, Adriana. As far as I'm concerned, it's a declaration of war."

But Adriana knew that the war had started the moment she'd been sent to work with this man, and despite what she'd told herself all these weeks, despite what she'd so desperately wanted to believe, she'd already lost.

Pato couldn't sleep, and he could *always* sleep.

This was one more thing that had never happened to him before Adriana had walked into his life and turned it inside out. He'd entertained a number of very detailed ideas about how he'd enjoy making her pay for that as he sprawled there in his decidedly empty bed—none of them particularly conducive to rest.

Damn her.

It was her insistence that she was, in fact, all the things the jackals called her that had him acting so outside his own parameters, he knew. It was maddening. Pato had handled any number of women over the years who had used their supposed fragility as a tool to try to manipulate him. He could have piloted a yacht across the sea of tears that had been cried on or near him, all by women angling for his affection, his protection, his money or his name—whatever they thought they could get.

He'd never been the slightest bit moved.

Adriana, by contrast, wanted nothing from him save his good behavior. She was appalled that he'd touched her, kissed her, made her forget herself. She'd now offered herself to him twice while making it perfectly clear that doing so was an act of great sacrifice on her part. A terrible sacrifice she would lower herself to suffer through, *even after* he'd brought her to a screaming, sobbing climax more than once.

She was killing him.

No wonder he was wide-awake in the middle of the night and storming through his rooms in a fury. If he'd been possessed of the ego of a lesser man, she might very well have deflated it by now. He'd even altered his behavior to please her. He, Pato, Playboy Prince, tabloid sensation and scandal magnet, hadn't even glanced at another woman unless it was specifically to annoy Adriana, since he didn't seem to be able to do without the way she took him to task.

He was like a lovesick puppy. He was disgusted with himself.

And he would never be able to fly on that plane again without being haunted by her. Her taste, her silken legs draped over his back, her gorgeous cries. He cursed into the dark room, but it didn't help.

The list of things he shouldn't have done grew longer every day, but tasting the heat of her, making her shatter around him, *twice,* was at the very top. It wasn't only that he'd tasted her at last and it had knocked him sideways, or that it had taken every shred of willpower he possessed to keep himself from driving into her and making her his in every possible way right there and then, again and again until they both collapsed. It wasn't only that he'd been unable to stop thinking about the fact that he was more than likely the first man to pleasure her, which made a wholly uncharacteristic barbarian stir to life inside him and beat at his chest in primitive masculine triumph. That was all bad enough.

But it went much deeper than that, and Pato knew it.

He'd known it while they were still in the air. He'd known it when he'd started telling her things he never spoke about, ever. He'd known it when the plane had finally landed and he'd sent her off in a separate car and had found himself standing on the tarmac, staring at her disappearing taillights and wanting things he couldn't have.

He'd known for some time, if he was honest, but tonight it had all come into sharp and unmistakable focus.

Pato didn't simply want her in his bed.

He *liked* her. She made him laugh, she challenged him and she wasn't the least bit in awe of him. From the very start, she'd treated him as if she expected him to be the educated, intelligent, capable man he was supposed to be rather than the airy dilettante he played so well. He wanted to teach her every last sensual trick he'd ever learned, and bathe them both in that scalding heat of hers. He wanted to prove to her that the passion that flared between them was rare and good. He wanted to take away the pressure of all that family history she wore about her neck like an albatross.

Worst of all, most damning and most dangerous, he wanted to be that better man she deserved.

"It isn't even my dirt, but I'm covered in it," she'd said tonight, breaking the heart he didn't have all over again, and he'd wanted nothing more than to be the one who showed her that she had never been anything but beautiful and clean, all the way through. Pato never should have let himself get lost in the fantasy that he might be that man. He wasn't. There was no possibility that he could be anything to her, and couldn't allow himself to forget that again.

Not until the game he and Lenz had played for all these years reached its conclusion. He couldn't break the faith his brother had placed in him all those years ago. He couldn't break the vow he'd made. He wouldn't.

And he'd never been even remotely tempted to do so before.

Pato found himself on one of his balconies that looked out over the water to the mainland beyond and the city nestled there on the lakeshore. His eyes drifted toward the sparkling lights of the old city, the ancient quarter that had sprawled over the highest hill since the first thatched cottages were built there in medieval times. It was filled with museums and grand old houses, narrow little lanes dating back centuries and so many of Kitzinia's blue-blooded nobles in their luxurious, historic villas. And he knew precisely where the Righetti villa stood on the finest street in the quarter, one of the kingdom's most famous and most visited landmarks.

But tonight he didn't think about his murdered ancestor or Almado Righetti's plot to turn the kingdom over to foreign enemies, all in service to long-ago wars. It was only the house where she lived, where he imagined her as wide-awake as he was, as haunted by him as he was by her. He didn't care what her surname was. He didn't care if this was history repeating itself. He certainly didn't care about the malicious gossip of others.

The ways he wanted her almost scared him. Almost.

And of all the things he couldn't have while this game played on, he understood that she was going to hurt the worst. She already did.

Pato slammed his fist against the thick stone balustrade. Hard. As if that might wake him up, restore him to himself. It did nothing but make his knuckles ache, and it didn't make him any less alone.

He hated this game, but he couldn't lose his focus. There was one week left until the wedding, and she'd served her purpose. He had to let her go.

CHAPTER SEVEN

ADRIANA WALKED INTO the palace the following morning on shaky legs, trying with all her might to feel completely unaffected by what had happened the night before. And if she couldn't quite feel it, to *appear* as if she did. Cool. Calm. Professional. Not riddled with anxiety, her body still humming with leftover desire.

"I wanted to know how you tasted," she could hear him say, as if he whispered it into her ear. Her skin prickled at the memory.

Nothing had changed, she assured herself, save her understanding of her own weakness and her ability to tell herself lies. And nothing *would* change, because this was Pato. Careless, promiscuous, thoughtless, undependable for the whole of his adult life, and proud of it besides. No depth, she reminded herself. No conscience and no shame. Those hints she'd seen of another man—that ruthless power, that dark focus, that devastating gentleness—weren't him.

They couldn't be him.

And the things he'd said, which she could still feel running through her like something electric... well. She'd lost herself in a sensual storm. She'd never experienced anything like it before and she'd decided it was entirely possible she'd made it all seem much more intense than it had been. Pato had made her sob and writhe and fall to pieces. He'd made her body sing for him as if she were no more than an instrument—and well he should. *Passion,* he'd called it, and he would know. Sex was his occupation, his art. He was a master.

He'd mastered her without even trying very hard.

It was no wonder she'd concocted some fantasy around that, she told herself as she made her way down the gleaming marble hall that led to Pato's office. He did things like this—like *her*—all the time. The number of women who fantasized about him was no doubt astronomical, and none of them hung about the palace, clinging to his ankles. Nor would she.

She would be perfectly serene, she chanted to herself as she let herself into his office. Efficient and competent. And she wouldn't verbally spar with him anymore, as he obviously viewed it as a form of flirtation, and she found it far too easy to slip into, putting herself at risk. Last night was a mistake, never to be repeated. No conversation was necessary, no embarrassing postmortem. It was done. She marched around the quietly opulent office, turning on lights and arranging the papers he wouldn't read on his desk. The two of them would simply...move forward.

Or so Adriana told herself, over and over, as she waited for him to appear.

He didn't come. She waited, she lectured herself more sternly, and still he failed to saunter in, disheveled and lazy and wearing something that violated every possible palace protocol, the way he usually did. When Adriana realized he was going to miss his engagement with the Kitzinian Red Cross—after what she'd gone through to get him back into the country, specifically to meet with them—she braced herself, smoothed her hands over the very conservative suit she'd chosen this morning, which was in no way protective armor, and set off through the palace to find him.

Pato's bed, she was relieved to find when she made it to his bedroom, was empty.

It was only then, while she stared at the rumpled sheets and the indentation in the pillows where his head must have been at some point last night, that Adriana admitted to herself that maybe she was a little *too* relieved. That maybe it had hurt to imagine that he could have carried on with his usual depravity after she'd left him last night.

You are nothing but another instrument, she reminded herself harshly, amazed at her capacity for self-delusion. *And he happens to be a remarkably talented musician—no doubt because he practices so very, very often.*

If only she could make that sink in. If only she could make that traitorous part of her, the part that insisted on wild fantasies and childish hope no matter how many times it was crushed out of her, believe it.

"You look disappointed," Pato drawled from the doorway behind her. Adriana whirled around to face him, her heart leaping out of her chest. "Shall I ring a few bored socialites and have them fill up the bed? Just think of all the sanctimonious lectures you could deliver."

He sounded the way he looked this morning: dangerous. Edgy. Dark and something like grim. Adriana's breath tangled in her throat.

Pato was draped against the doorjamb, looking as boneless as he did rough around his gorgeous edges. His eyes glittered, too dark to shine like gold today, and he hadn't bothered to shave. His hair stood about his head in a careless mess, and he was wearing an open, button-down shirt over those ancient jeans he preferred, she'd often thought, because they molded so tightly to his perfectly formed body. He looked moody and formidable, that ruthless power he usually concealed a black cloud around him today, making it impossible for Adriana to pretend she'd imagined it.

And the way he was looking at her made her heart stutter.

She'd been so sure that she was prepared to see him again. She wasn't.

Her whole body simply shuddered into a blazing, embarrassing heat at the sight of him. She felt as if she'd been lit on fire. Her nipples hardened as her breasts swelled against her bra. Her belly tightened, while her core melted into that hot, needy ache. Her skin prickled with awareness, and she could feel the dark heat of his gaze all the way through her, from the nape of her neck to the soles of her feet. Not ten minutes ago she'd vowed she wouldn't spar with him anymore, but she understood in a flash of insight that it was that or simply surrender to this wildness inside her—and she wasn't that far gone, surely. Not yet.

"I'm relieved, actually," she managed to say, making her voice as brisk as she could. "The last thing I wanted to do today was troll about your usual dens of iniquity, looking for you in the dregs of last night's parties, especially when you are expected to charm the Red Cross in less than hour."

He looked at her for a long moment, his beautiful face hard and his eyes dark, and yet she had the strangest notion that he was in some kind of pain. She had to grit her teeth to keep herself from doing something stupid, like trying to reach out to him. Like imagining that she of all people could see beneath his surface to the far more complicated man beneath.

Such hubris, a voice inside her hissed, *and we all know what comes after pride like yours. Like night follows day.*

"It's amazing," Pato said in a low voice, something in it raising the fine hairs on the back of her neck. "It's as if you never wrapped your legs around my neck and let me taste you. You may not remember it, Adriana, but I do."

Adriana went utterly still.

She should have anticipated this. She should have known. It had been the same when she was seventeen. She could still remember with perfect clarity the faces of all her schoolmates who'd gathered around to point and stare and laugh as she'd walked out of that party alone. Used and humiliated. She could still remember the name they'd called her snaking along with her like a shadow, following her, connected to her, the truth of her as far as they'd been concerned. Inevitable.

The Righetti whore.

Pato was only one person, not a crowd of cruel teenagers, and yet she recognized that this was worse. Much, much worse. She could feel it deep inside, in parts of her that pack of kids had never touched.

But she'd be damned if he'd see her cry again, Adriana thought then with a sharp flash of defiance. She'd rather he executed her alongside

Almado Righetti's ghost in the old castle keep than show him one more tear.

"Is this the part where you call me a whore?" she asked, her stomach in a hard knot but her voice crisp. Her head high. "You're not doing it right. It works much better when mixed with public humiliation, so you can get the satisfaction of watching me walk a little gauntlet of shame. Would you like me to assemble a crowd? We can start over when they arrive."

Pato didn't move, but his eyes went completely black. Frigid and furious at once. Adriana crossed her arms over her chest and refused to cower or cringe. That deep defiance felt like strength, sweeping through her, making her stand tall. She would never bow her head in shame again. Never. Not even for a prince.

"If you want to call me names, feel free to do it to my face," she told him. "But I should warn you, I won't fall to pieces. I've survived far worse than you."

It shouldn't have been possible for his eyes to flash even darker, but they did, and she could feel the pulse of his temper rolling off him in waves.

She told herself it didn't bother her in the least, because it shouldn't. It couldn't.

"You think you're ready to go to war with me, Adriana?" he asked, that mild tone sounding alarms inside her, sending a little chill racing down her back. "I told you what would happen if you used that word again."

"Here's a news flash, Your Royal Highness," she snapped, ignoring the alarms, the chill, that look on his face. "I've been at war since the day I was born. I'm hardly afraid of one more battle, especially with a man best known for the revealing cut of his swimming costume and his ability to consume so much alcohol it ought to put him in a coma." She eyed him while a muscle she'd never seen before flared in his jaw. "Is that what today's little display of temper is all about? You're drunk?"

Pato straightened from the door, and her heart kicked at her in a sudden panic, not quite as tough as she was trying to appear. Adriana almost took an instinctive step back, but forced herself to stop. To stand still. He looked nothing less than predatory and the last thing she wanted to do was encourage him to give chase. Because he would, she knew on some primal level. In this mood he might do anything.

"No," he growled in a voice like gravel, when she'd almost forgotten she'd asked him a question. "I'm not drunk. Not even a little."

She didn't like the way he watched her then. Panic and awareness twisted inside her, sending out a shower of sparks, but Adriana didn't let herself back down. She wasn't going to break. Not this time. Not here.

"Perhaps you should consider getting drunk, then," she suggested icily. "It might improve your disposition."

She didn't see him move, and then he was right there in front of her, his hand on her jaw and his eyes so tortured, so dark, as he gazed down at her. Adriana didn't understand what was happening. The things he was saying, that dangerous tone of voice, his dark demeanor—but then she looked in his eyes and she wanted to cry. And not for herself.

"What's wrong?" she whispered.

Something she didn't understand flashed through those eyes. Then he bent his head and brushed his lips across hers. It was soft and light, hardly a kiss at all, and even so, Adriana felt it as if he'd wrapped both hands around her heart and squeezed tight. Her eyes closed of their own accord, and she felt the sweetness of it work through her, warming her, making her feel as if she glowed.

And then he let go of her, though he didn't step back, and when she looked at him he was that dark, edgy stranger again. His mouth was severe as he gazed at her, a grim line without the faintest possibility of any curve. Much less anything sweet.

"For the first time since you walked through the door and started ordering me around," he said quietly, "I feel like myself."

Adriana stared at him for a long moment. He looked back at her, that wicked mouth unrecognizable, those beautiful eyes so terribly dark and filled with things she didn't understand—but she understood this. He didn't need to call her names. He didn't need to stoop to the level of seventeen-year-olds. He was a royal prince. He could do it with a glance, a single sentence.

She had to stop imagining that anything would ever be different.

"If you want to be rid of me, Pato," she said, fighting to keep her voice cool and her head high, "you don't have to play these cruel little games.

All you have to do is dismiss me, and you could have done that with a text. No unpleasant scene required."

He reached over and ran the back of one hand along her cheek, his knuckles slightly swollen, and Adriana fought to keep from jerking her head away. His touch was confusingly tender. It slid through her like honey. And it was at complete odds with everything he was saying.

"That's the first time you've used my name," he said, as if it shook him. And Adriana wanted to lean into him, to turn her head and kiss his hand, as if this was about affection.

But she knew better. This was another game. It couldn't be anything else—and she was finished playing. No matter what she thought she saw in his eyes then, as if using his name had been some kind of invocation. As if it had changed something.

"I'll take that as a yes, I'm dismissed," she said somehow, and moved to step around him. The need to escape, to flee this place and him and never look back, was like a drumbeat inside her skin. "I'll leave my formal resignation letter on the desk in your office."

But he reached out and took her arm as he had

once before in London, holding her against his side though they faced different directions.

"Adriana," he whispered, as if her name hurt him.

It hurt her.

But all this would pass. It would, it always did. All she had to do was walk out the door, and she'd never be allowed in his presence again. It wasn't as if she could work for Lenz again, not now. Her access to the palace would be revoked, and she'd never have to worry about her outsize reactions to Pato, her insatiable hunger for him. All that would fade away as if it had never happened, as if he'd never been anything more than a face on a glossy magazine. And she would move far away from Kitzinia, to a place where no one would recognize her name or her ancestors' faces in hers, and someday, she thought—*prayed*—she might even forget that she'd fallen in love with him without ever meaning to.

Everything inside her went still then. Quiet. The truth she'd been avoiding for much too long was like a hush, stealing through her, changing everything, making sure she would leave here, leave him, in tatters.

But then she supposed that, too, had always been inevitable. History had repeated itself, and he was right, it might kill her. But not where he could watch, she told herself fiercely. Not where he could see how far she'd fallen.

"Thank you, Your Royal Highness," she said, jerking her arm from his grasp, amazed that she sounded so calm. So controlled, as if her whole world hadn't shuddered to a halt and then altered forever. "This has been an educational experience. I particularly enjoyed your need to destroy the entire royal family, living and dead, in my esteem." She aimed a hard smile at him. "Rest assured, I now think as little of your family as you do of mine."

He met her gaze then, and what she saw on his face sliced into her, making her feel as if she might shake apart where she stood. Making her think she already had.

"Don't," he said, as he had in the car that day. That was all, and yet she felt it everywhere.

But his pain wasn't her problem, she told herself harshly. She couldn't let it matter.

"I didn't need to know any of that," she whispered fiercely. His secrets, that tempting glimpse of his inner self. As if any of it was real, or hers. She'd known it would lead nowhere good, and she was right. "And why would you risk telling me? I could walk out of here today and sell that story to the tabloids."

The way he looked at her didn't make any sense. It made her heart thud hard against her ribs. It made her eyes go blurry.

"You won't."

"You have no reason to think that. You don't know me. You don't even like me."

His smile was faint, like a ghost. "I trust you, Adriana."

It was sad how much she wished he did, despite everything. She was such a terrible, gullible fool. Such a deep and abiding disappointment to herself. Because he was still playing her. She knew it. She was one instrument among many, and he didn't know how to do anything else.

"Or," she said slowly, as the ugly truth of it penetrated even her thick skull, the misery crashing over her, into her, making her voice too thick, "you know perfectly well that the last person in the world anyone would believe when it came to accusations of promiscuity is me."

"Don't," he said again, his voice harsher.

And this time when he pulled her to him, he turned her so she came up hard against his chest, and then he held her face in his hands and kissed her. Ravenous and raw. Uncontrolled.

Dangerous.

And Adriana couldn't help herself. She kissed him back.

He slanted his head and she met him, kissing him with all the passion he'd showed her, all the love she hadn't wanted to admit she felt for him. The pain, the misery. Her foolish hopes. She held back nothing. She wrapped her arms around his neck and let him bend her backward, as if this was the happy ending to some kind of fairy tale instead of a sad goodbye at the close of a story even Adriana had known would end like this. Exactly like this, in dismissal and disgrace.

Pato kissed her again and again, as if he was as desperate, as torn, as she was. As if he felt what she did when she knew very well he didn't. He couldn't. He kissed her so thoroughly that she knew she would pretend he did, that it would be the fire she warmed herself near in all the lonely days to follow, and she kissed him back with the same ferocity so she could remember that, too.

But too soon he pulled away, still holding her face in his hands. He looked at her for a long moment, his eyes gleaming that darker gold that made her shiver deep inside, and then he stroked her cheeks with his thumbs, as if memorizing her.

Adriana didn't say a word. She couldn't. But she knew it was time to go, before she found she couldn't.

She pulled in a shuddering breath, and when she stepped back, Pato's gaze went stormy and his jaw flexed—but he dropped his hands and let her.

It was the hardest thing Adriana had ever had to do. It made her bones ache as if she was breaking them, but she did it. She wrenched herself away from him and turned toward the door.

And then stopped dead.

Because Lenz stood there, staring at them both in appalled disbelief.

Adriana made a small sound of distress, almost too low to hear, and Pato wanted nothing more than to put himself bodily between her and whatever attacked her—even if it was his brother. Even worse, if it was him.

But he couldn't. He certainly hadn't today. He didn't now, and he thought he loathed himself.

For a moment, they all stood there, frozen in place.

"Excuse me, Your Royal—" Adriana began, but Lenz interrupted her.

"I didn't give her to you so you could make her one of your bedmates, Pato." He threw the accusation into the room, his face a work of thunder. But Pato watched Adriana and the way she simply stood there, her spine achingly straight and her hands in fists at her sides. "What the hell are you thinking?"

Pato said nothing. He saw Adriana tremble slightly, and had to fight the need to pull her back against him, to protect her from this. He hated that she thought he was like those jackals who had hounded her all these years. He hated that she believed he thought so little of what had happened between them. He hated all of this.

And yet he had no choice, he reminded himself bitterly. It didn't matter that he had the taste of her in his mouth, that he would have held her there forever if she hadn't pulled away. He had to let her go.

"Enough," he snapped when Lenz opened his mouth again. Pato met his brother's eyes. Hard and unyielding. "This is not a conversation Adriana needs to take part in. Why don't you step aside and let her go?"

It appeared to dawn on Lenz that this was not a request. His eyes narrowed, but he walked stiffly into the room, leaving the exit clear.

Pato willed Adriana to look at him one last time—to let him study that beautiful face of hers once more—but he wasn't surprised that she didn't. The moment Lenz stopped moving, she left. She walked out of Pato's bedroom the way she'd walked into it, her head high and her back straight, and she didn't look back or break her stride.

And Pato stood there, listening to the sound of her heels against the polished floors until even that disappeared. And that was it. She was gone. He'd done his goddamned duty.

"You didn't have to sleep with her!" Lenz declared, sounding fierce and protective, which made Pato feel that much more hollow. "She deserves better than that!"

"By all means, brother, let's talk about what Adriana deserves," Pato murmured dangerously. "The crown prince installs her in the position usually allocated to his mistresses, and keeps her there for years. And then his dirty playboy brother takes his sordid turn. And we planned it that way, because we knew exactly what would happen if we brought the last Righetti girl into this game. Does she deserve any of that?"

Lenz stared at him. "What is she to you?" he asked after a long moment.

"She is nothing to me," Pato replied, his voice harsh. "Because *nothing* is the only thing I am allowed. *Nothing* is my stock in trade. I am useless, faithless, untrustworthy, and most of all, a great and continuing disgrace to my royal blood." He held Lenz's gaze for a taut breath. "Don't worry, brother. I know who I am."

Lenz looked pale then.

"Pato," he said carefully, as if he was afraid of what Pato's response might be. "We are finally in the endgame. We've worked too hard to get here. Didn't you tell me this yourself only weeks ago?"

Pato scraped his hands over his face as if that

could change the growing hollowness inside him. As if anything could.

"I know what I promised." But he didn't look at Lenz. He felt unbalanced, half-drunk, and he knew it was Adriana. She'd crippled him, and she thought he didn't care. It was almost funny. "I have no intention of breaking my vow. I haven't yet, have I?"

Lenz stared at him, lifting one hand to stroke his mouth, clearly mulling over the right approach to a thorny problem he hadn't seen coming. Pato almost laughed then. This was why Lenz would make the perfect king. He could detach, step back, consider all outcomes. Pato, by contrast, couldn't seem to do anything but seethe and rage. Especially today.

"We picked Adriana because of her name, yes," Lenz said after several moments passed, his voice carefully diplomatic once again. "But she's special. I know it. I—"

Pato laughed then, a rusty blade of a sound that stopped his brother flat.

"We're not going to stand about like pimpled schoolboys and compare notes," he said in a tone that brooked no argument. "We'll be the only people in this petty kingdom who do not find it necessary to pick over her body like so many carrion crows."

For a moment, that simply hung there. Then Lenz blinked.

"Oh," he said in a curious voice, a new light in his eyes as he looked at Pato. "I didn't realize."

"She's out of this," Pato said, ignoring that. "She isn't coming back."

Lenz studied him. "Is that wise?" he asked quietly. "Can we afford a deviation from the plan at this point? The wedding—"

"Is in a week, I know." Pato couldn't hide the bleakness that washed over him then. He didn't try. "And she's out of this. She's free. If she deserves anything, it's that."

Lenz's brows rose, but he only nodded. "Fair enough."

Pato smiled then, though it was too sharp, and he understood that he was not himself. That he might never be himself again. That Adriana was gone and he was emptier than he'd been before, and he wasn't sure he could live with it the way he knew he must. But he smiled anyway.

"How is the king's health?" he asked, because Lenz was right. This was the end of this game, and he'd agreed years ago to play it. There was no changing that now, even if he'd changed the plan.

"The same," Lenz said. He didn't smile. He only looked tired. "The ministers are beginning to press him. It might happen sooner than we thought."

Pato nodded. It was exactly as they'd planned. It turned out they were good at this, this dance of high-stakes deception and royal intrigue.

He sickened himself.

"Then I suppose we play on," he said wearily.

Lenz's gaze was sad. "We always do."

Adriana walked through her family's villa slowly, taking the time to really look around her as she did. She couldn't remember the last time she'd paid attention to all the familiar things in front of her, which she'd somehow stopped seeing over the years. The graceful rooms, the antique furniture. The art still on the walls and the places where art had been removed and sold in the leaner years. All the *things* that made up a Kitzinian pedigree, a certain station in Kitzinian society, even a tarnished one. Collections of china in carved wood cabinets. Beautiful rugs, hand-tiled floors, mosaics lining the fountain in the center courtyard.

Coats of arms, priceless statues and pieces of pottery handed down across centuries.

And in the small parlor in the farthest corner of the villa, the one no one talked about and never visited by accident, were the trio of portraits. The faces of the women whose choices hundreds of years ago had sentenced Adriana to infamy in the present.

"What they call you reflects far more on them than on you," Pato had said. She couldn't get his words out of her head.

Her father might hate their family history, Adriana thought as she stood in the musty room, but he still felt called upon to preserve it. And so the portraits hung on the walls of the villa instead of being packed away in the attic or burned in the back gardens. This was his duty to the Righetti legacy, however shameful he found it.

Adriana pulled open the heavy drapes to let the light in, and then stared up at the three great temptresses of old Kitzinia sitting there so prettily in their frames. The Righetti whores, lined up in chronological order. The harlots Carolina, Maria and Francesca.

And, of course, Adriana herself, though she, like

her great-aunt Sandrine, could not expect to be rendered in oils and hung in museums. Times had changed.

She couldn't help the small laugh that escaped her. *She* didn't feel much like a notorious whore in the comfortable jeans and soft magenta sweater she'd tugged on when she'd arrived home from the palace. She studied the faces of the women before her, seeing herself in the shape of Carolina's brow, the color of Maria's hair and the curve of Francesca's lips. None of them looked particularly like slinking sexpots, either. They simply looked like young women somewhere around Adriana's age, all smiling, all bright-eyed, all pretty.

Don't lock yourself in their prison, Pato had said.

Maybe, Adriana thought, staring at the portraits but remembering the way he'd held her when she cried, they'd simply fallen in love.

She sat down heavily in the nearest chair, her own heart beating hard in her chest as if she'd run up a hill. How had that possibility never occurred to her before? Why had she always believed that she was descended from a line of women who were, for all intents and purposes, callous prostitutes?

Maybe they were in love.

It rang in her like a revolution.

The Righetti family had always kept their own copies of these portraits, and Adriana remembered being herded into this room by her grandmother after church on Sundays, as her aunts had been before her. Her grandmother had droned on about purity and morals, while Adriana had stood there feeling increasingly cross that her brothers were allowed to entertain themselves elsewhere.

The lecture had been repeated with increasing frequency throughout her adolescence, which was when Adriana had discovered the truth about her grandfather's younger sister, the lovely old woman with sparkling eyes who lived in France and whose name was only ever spoken in distaste. And Adriana had internalized every word of her grandmother's lecture. She'd accepted the fact that she was dirty, tainted. Ruined before she began. She'd never questioned a word of it.

"Don't use their weapons on yourself," Pato had said so fiercely, as if it had angered him to hear her talk about herself like that. As if the casual way she hated herself, her easy acceptance of the idea

that she was the dirty thing others called her, was what was upsetting.

Not her. Not her name. Not what had happened between them.

And she realized then, as she sat in the presence of the women who'd supposedly ruined her, that she couldn't do it anymore. That well of ugliness she'd spent her whole life drawing from simply wasn't there in her gut the way it always had been. In its place, she thought in some astonishment, was that defiance she'd called on at the palace—that strength she hadn't known she had.

She looked at the Righetti women, at their mysterious smiles and the sparkle in their eyes, and she knew something else, too. These women hadn't been ashamed. They hadn't torn themselves apart in penance for their sins. Adriana knew for a fact that each and every one of them had died of old age, in their beds. These were not meek, placating women. They'd been the favorite lovers of kings and princes in times when that meant they'd wielded great power and political influence. They'd made their own rules.

And so, by God, would Adriana.

At some point she realized that tears were flow-ing down her cheeks. Was this joy? Heartbreak? Despair? How could she keep track of the wild emotions that clamored inside of her? Adriana knew only that she loved him. She loved Pato, and she wasn't ashamed of it, either. She didn't know how she would tell her father what had happened, or what she'd do next, but she couldn't hate herself for this.

She *wouldn't* hate herself for this.

Adriana had thought for a moment that she might have a heart attack when she'd turned to see Lenz standing there in Pato's doorway, when she'd seen that shocked look on his face. But seeing him there, standing next to his brother, had made everything very clear. *"I don't think you love him,"* Pato had told her, and he was right. Lenz had been kind to her, no matter what his ulterior motives, and she'd been so desperate to prove to him that she wasn't *that kind* of Righetti. She'd mistaken her gratitude for something more.

But Pato had changed her, she realized now, gazing at that trinity of women before her as she wiped at her cheeks. What had happened on that plane had altered everything. He had wanted her, and he'd encouraged her to want him back. He hadn't used her; if anything, she'd used him. Twice. And the things he'd said to her had knocked down walls inside her she'd never known were there.

It didn't matter what came after that. It didn't matter if he regretted opening up to her the way he had. It didn't matter that he'd rejected her today, or that it had hurt her terribly.

It didn't even matter if she never saw him again, though that possibility broke her heart. He'd given her a gift she could never repay, she understood now. She wasn't sure she ever would have got there on her own. He'd showed her how.

He'd set her free.

Later, Adriana sat on the wide sill at her open bedroom windows, looking out at the stretch of the kingdom below her, gleaming in the crisp afternoon light.

She watched the ferries cutting through the crystal blue lake toward the cities on the far shore, racing the pleasure boats with their white sails taut in the breeze. She let her eyes trace the graceful lines of the palace, the gentle bow of the causeway that connected it to the mainland, and the towering Alps all around. There was nothing keeping her here besides sentiment. She could go back to university, collect another degree. She could travel abroad the way she'd always meant to do. There was no reason she had to stay here. None at all.

And even so, even now, she found it hard to imagine leaving.

Adriana heard the motorcycle long before she saw it. It was brash and loud, shouting its way through the streets of the old city. Louder and louder it roared, until it whipped around the corner at the end of the lane, charged down her street in an obnoxious cloud of noise and then stopped directly below her windows.

Her heart slammed against her chest.

Pato tilted back his head and glanced up, pulling off his helmet and piercing her with a long, hard look. Adriana couldn't seem to move. His expression was serious, unsmiling, and he paused there, one foot on the ground, handling the sleek black machine beneath him with an easy, unconscious grace.

And his eyes gleamed gold for all that they were grave.

She didn't know how long they stared at each other. The whole city could have gathered around, jeering and pointing, and it wouldn't have registered. There was only Pato. Here, beneath her window. *Here.*

And then he smiled, and she felt it everywhere, like that hungry mouth of his, demanding and hot. *So hot.* She felt herself flush red.

Pato crooked his finger at her, arrogant and sure. He looked anything but careless. He was impossibly powerful, decidedly male, every inch of him a prince though he wore jeans and a black T-shirt that made love to his lean and chiseled body, and held that lethally beautiful machine between his legs.

Adriana scowled at him, because she wanted to melt, and saw his eyes heat in response. He crooked his finger again, with even more lazy command this time, and she shook her head.

"You dismissed me for a reason, or so I assume," she said, in a reasonable attempt at her usual brisk tone, as if she didn't care that he was here. That he'd come when she'd thought she'd never see him again. "You can't change your mind back and forth on a whim and expect—"

"Adriana," he said, and the sound of her name in his mouth like that, so quiet and so serious in the narrow, cobblestone street, made her fall silent. Pato didn't smile or laugh; he didn't show her that grin of his, though his golden gaze was bright. "Come here."

CHAPTER EIGHT

ADRIANA STEPPED INTO the street, pulling the door to the villa shut behind her, and felt Pato's eyes on her long before she turned to face him. His golden gaze seared into her, brighter than the afternoon around them, making her heart pick up speed.

"That machine is much too loud," she told him, the stern tone surprising her even as she used it. His mouth curved in the corner. "It's noise pollution and you are a—"

"Get on the bike." His voice was as commanding as that crook of his finger had been, and that gleam in his gaze had gone hotter, more challenging.

"I no longer serve you, Your Royal Highness," she said primly, though her heart was beating too fast, too hard, and she could see the way he studied the color on her cheeks in that lazy way of his. "At your pleasure or otherwise."

He still didn't smile, though the gleam in his eyes suggested it, and then he reached out and hooked his fingers in the waistband of her jeans. Her skin ignited at his touch, making her forget what she'd been saying. The burn of it went deep when he tugged her close, so close her head fell back and all she could see was him.

"I was cruel," Pato said, his voice dark. "Chastising me won't change that, though perhaps it makes you feel better. But you can admit you want me anyway." His gaze was steady. He wasn't toying with her. He knew. "There's no shame in it."

Adriana went white, then red. Shock. Embarrassment. Fury.

"I don't know what makes you think—"

Her breath left her in a rush when his fingers moved gently over the soft skin just beneath her waistband, teasing her. Tormenting her. Making whatever she was about to say a lie.

"Adriana." His voice was pure velvet now, wrapped around steel. "Get on the bike." He held out a helmet.

And she'd known she would, since the moment he'd appeared outside her windows, hadn't she? Why had she pretended otherwise? It wasn't as if Pato was fooled. It wasn't as if she'd fooled herself.

But there was admitting she loved him in the privacy of her own head, and then there was proving it beyond any doubt—announcing it out loud. And she was fairly certain that climbing up on the back of that motorcycle mere hours after he'd ripped out her heart, sacked her and undone three years of attempted rehabilitation to the Righetti reputation by kissing her like that in front of his brother constituted shouting it at the top of her lungs. *To* him.

She either loved him or she was a masochistic fool, Adriana thought then. Perhaps both.

But she donned the helmet and got on the bike.

Pato headed away from the palace, out of the city and up into the foothills.

Adriana clung to his back, luxuriating in the feel of all his corded, lean strength so close to her and the wind rushing around them. She was pressed into him, her arms wrapped around his waist, her breasts against his back, her legs on either side of his astride the motorcycle he operated as if it was an extension of himself. She felt surrounded by him, connected to him, a part of him.

It was either heaven or hell, she wasn't sure which. But she wanted it to never end.

Eventually he turned off the main roads and followed smaller, less-traveled ones around the far side of the lake, winding his way to a small cottage nestled in a hollow, looking out over a secluded cove. Adriana climbed off the motorcycle when he brought it to a roaring stop, her legs shaky beneath her. Her body felt too big suddenly, as if she'd outgrown her skin. As if it hurt to sever herself from him. She pulled off her helmet and handed it over, feeling somewhat shy. Overwhelmed.

Pato's gaze met hers as he removed his helmet. His mouth moved into a small curve, and she flushed. Again. She felt restless. Hectic and hot, and the way he looked at her didn't help. There might not be shame in wanting him, but there was too much need, and all of it too obvious now that she'd admitted it. Now that she'd stopped pretending.

And all she could seem to do was ache.

Adriana turned to look at the water instead, breathing in the peaceful, fragrant air. Pine and sun, summer flowers and the deep, quiet woods. It was still in ways the city never was. She watched the water lap gently at the rocks at the bottom of the sloping yard, blue and clear and pretty.

It made the odd tension inside her ease. Shift. Turn into something else entirely. They could have been worlds away from the city, the palace, she thought. They could have been anyone, anywhere. Anonymous and free.

"What is this place?" she asked, her voice sounding strange in the quiet, odd in her own mouth.

"It's my best kept secret." Pato stepped away from the motorcycle and shoved his thick hair back from his forehead. The movement made his T-shirt pull tight over that marvelous torso of his, and Adriana's mouth went dry. The gleam in his gaze when she met it again told her he could tell. "I come here to be alone."

She couldn't let herself think about that too closely. She wanted it to mean much, much more than it did.

"More secrets," she murmured instead. His gaze seemed to burn hotter the longer he looked at her, more intense. She tried to shake off the strangeness, the shakiness. All that want and need, and no barriers to contain them. It made her feel off-kilter. Vulnerable. *Alive.* "Private stories, secret cottages. Who knew the overexposed prince had so much to hide? Or that you were capable of hiding anything in the first place?"

He moved closer, and she felt that sizzling current leap between them and then work its way through her, lighting her up the way it always did. The way *he* always did. Fire upon fire, a chain reaction, sweeping over her unchecked until she was molten all the way through. As needy and as desperate as if he was already touching her. As if this morning had never happened.

But it had, and Adriana understood, even through the sweet ache of all that fire between them, that it would again. He wasn't hers. He could never be hers.

And yet she'd come with him, anyway. She'd barely hesitated.

Maybe, like the Righetti women who came before her, it was time she loved what she had for as long as she had it, instead of mourning what she might have had, were she braver. Pato had told her this was passion, this thing that flared between them. She wanted to explore it. She wanted to know what he meant. She wanted *him.*

It didn't feel like surrender to admit that. There was no shame. It felt like a hard-won victory.

"You weren't what I expected," Pato said, as if the words were pulled from him, urgent and dark. Serious. "I've been hiding in plain sight for fifteen years and no one's ever seen me, any hint of me at all, until—"

Adriana turned to him and put her hand over his mouth, that beautiful mouth of his she'd felt devouring her very core, wicked and insinuating and warm to the touch. She felt his lips against her palm now, and the familiar punch of heat that roared through her and connected with that pulsing fire low in her belly.

She didn't want his secrets. Secrets came at too high a price, and she knew she'd pay a hefty one already. She wanted *him.* She wanted to throw herself in this fire at last, and who cared what burned?

"Don't," she whispered, and smiled at him. His gaze was dark on hers for a breath, and another. Then his lips curved against her palm.

Adriana pushed up on her toes, pressed her body flush against his *at last,* and took his mouth with hers. Claiming him here, now. While she could.

Pato met her instantly. He buried one hand in her hair and hauled her against him, and this time she was ready for him. She wrapped herself around him, shameless and abandoned, and let herself glory in it. He let out a sound that was halfway between a laugh and a curse, and then he was sweeping her up into his arms and heading toward the cottage.

"But—" she protested, though she went quiet when he looked down at her, his golden eyes hot and wild, making her shiver in anticipation as she hooked an arm around his hard shoulders.

"Rule number six," he growled, leaning down to nip at her nose. "Don't ever put on a sex show in the yard. Unless it's planned." He shifted her against his chest, holding her with one arm while he worked the door of the cottage with his free hand. "And if it's planned, there should be paparazzi at the ready, not horrified tourists out for a bit of pleasure boating."

Adriana frowned at him as he ducked into the cottage, barely taking notice of the place as he kicked the door closed behind him and carried her inside. She saw high beams and white walls, cozy furniture in bold colors. But she was far more interested in what he'd said.

"Exactly how many 'sex shows' have you participated in?" she demanded. "Planned or unplanned?"

"I don't think you really want me to answer that," he replied, laughter gleaming in those eyes of his now, mixing with all the fire and coiling inside her, tighter and tighter.

"More than five?" she asked, pushing it. Poking at him. *Flirting,* she understood now. She'd been flirting all this time. From the moment he'd opened his eyes and offered her a space in his crowded bed. "Ten? I imagine there would have to be quite a few to justify the making of rules and regulations."

Pato only laughed, and set her down on her feet slowly, letting her body slide down the length of his. Adriana melted against him, almost unable to stand on her own when he let go of her. She swayed slightly, and she didn't care that he could see how he affected her. She wanted him to see it.

"A gentleman doesn't count such things," he said, with a wicked quirk of his mouth. "That would be indelicate."

"Happily, you are no gentleman," she pointed out. "A prince, yes. But never a gentleman."

"Lucky you," he murmured, and then slid his hands under the hem of her whisper-soft sweater, directly onto the bare skin beneath.

Adriana's breath left her in a rush. Pato moved one hand around to the small of her back, and left the other where it was, big and delicious on her abdomen. Then he simply held her there, as if basking in the feel of her skin against his palms, her body between in his grasp.

"Listen to me," he said, and it took her a moment to pull herself out of her feverish little haze and focus on him again. When she did, his expression was serious. "I can't seem to resist you. But I don't think you're a whore, Adriana. I never did."

She felt gloriously free with his hands on her, with that fire burning so bright in her. With need lighting her up, making her pulse and glow.

"I don't care."

Pato shook his head impatiently. "I care. There are things you need to understand, things that are bigger than—"

"Later," she interrupted.

He frowned at her. So she reached down and grabbed the hem of her sweater herself, then pulled it up and off. She met his gaze as she tossed it aside, smiling slightly at the instant flash of heat there, and the way his hands tightened on her skin, as if he wasn't so controlled himself.

"Pato," she whispered. "I don't want to talk anymore."

He looked torn for a split second. Then that mouth of his curved into pure, male wickedness, and she knew the fire won. She felt it burn ever higher inside her, the flames licking all over her skin.

Pato stepped away from her and then reached back with one arm to tug that tight black T-shirt off his chest, throwing it on the floor near her sweater. This time, she could touch. Taste. This time she could lose herself in the sheer masculine perfection of that lean torso. She couldn't wait.

"Keep your eyes on me," he ordered when she reached for him, his golden gaze amused as it seared into her. "And no touching until I say otherwise."

The air inside the cottage seemed too tight, too hot. How could she keep from touching him? And why—? Pato only smiled.

"Surely," she managed to say, "the *point* is to touch. I feel certain that one of your ninety thousand supermodel lovers must have taught you that in all these years of your celebrated promiscuity."

"If there were ninety thousand supermodels," he said, grinning lazily at her, "they couldn't all be super, could they? I do have standards."

He laughed when she rolled her eyes. But when he looked at her, everything got gold and hot and desperate, and that ache in her bloomed into an open flame.

"The point," he murmured in that silken voice of his, making that flame reach higher and higher, "is to want this so badly you think you might die from it."

"Pato…"

She didn't know she'd said his name again until she saw the way his eyes darkened, then tracked over her body, resting on her breasts and the lilac bra she wore. She felt heavy. Desperate for his touch. Any touch at all.

"I want to know if you match again. I want you to show me." Slowly, so slowly, he lifted his gaze back to hers, and what she saw there made her pulse heat. "And then I want you naked, and if I do it myself I'll be inside you before I get those jeans over your hips and then we'll be done and Adriana?" She stared at him, so wild with heat she thought she might explode. Or die. Or both. His smile was dark and dangerous and she felt it in her toes. "We want this to last a little while."

Her throat was dry. Her heart was pounding. The

things she wanted whirled inside her, making her skin pull tight as if she might burst out of it.

"But what if I want to undress you?" she asked. Because she did. Almost more than she could bear. Because if she never had him again, she wanted to have this. As much of him as she could.

He touched her then, and she shuddered at the sheer joy of it. He ran his hand over her cheek, into her hair, and then held her there. Simply held her, and it made the need inside her turn into a white-hot surge of lightning.

"I told you this a long time ago," he said in that same darkly thrilling tone. "But I meant it. I like things my way."

He leaned closer then and brushed his mouth over hers, making goose bumps rise all over her body. She whispered a soft curse and Pato laughed against her mouth.

"And so will you," he promised.

She believed him.

He released her, then raised a dark, imperious brow.

Adriana hurriedly kicked off her shoes, grinning when he did the same. Then she unbuttoned her jeans and peeled them down her legs, feeling awkward until she saw the way he watched her, as if every millimeter of skin she revealed was a revelation.

And then she stood there before him, once again in nothing but her bra and panties. In matching lilac-colored lace.

Pato's smile had a dangerous edge to it. It worked its way into her pulse, making her shift restlessly from foot to foot. He stripped off his own jeans with a minimum of fuss, leaving him in nothing but another pair of those tight briefs that made him look edible.

And she wanted to taste him so badly it began to hurt.

Need made her clumsy. She forgot to be shy. She forgot she was inexperienced. She forgot everything but the man watching her, his gaze getting harder and more intense by the second.

Adriana unhooked her bra. When she pulled it away from her breasts, her nipples were already taut, and she heard Pato let out a sigh. Then she bent and tugged off her panties, and she heard him mutter something beneath his breath. And when she straightened she was naked, and he was looking at her as if she was something holy.

She felt beautiful. She felt like the temptress, the wanton she'd always been called, and when he looked at her like that, she was glad. Bold women lived in her blood, she knew that now, and watching the way his eyes moved over her, bathing her in golden fire, she finally felt as bold as they were. As free as he'd made her.

He took off his briefs, studied her for another long moment, as if committing the sight of her to memory, and then crooked his finger once more, that wicked smile taking over his mouth.

Adriana walked to him immediately, too desperate to mind his high-handedness. She sighed happily when his hands went to her waist, then smoothed down to her hips—and then he pulled her to him, tumbling them both down on the sofa and arranging her over his lap so she sat astride him.

"Be still," he told her when she squirmed against him, and it very nearly hurt her to stop, but she did it. Her heart beat so hard she could feel it in her temples.

For a moment, he only stared up at her.

She felt his hard thighs beneath her, and the hardest part of him pressed against her, making her hotter, wilder. Needier by the second. She saw the blazing heat in his eyes, the dark passion, and thought she could drown in that alone. He waited. He watched.

"Do you feel like you might die?" he asked, his voice a low whisper, teasing at her skin, moving through her body and making her tremble.

"I think I already did," she confessed.

His mouth curved. And then he leaned forward and sucked her nipple into his mouth without the slightest hesitation, all of that wet heat against the tender peak, and she was lost.

Pato didn't ask, she discovered quickly. He took.

He used his mouth and his tongue against the weight of her breasts, used the hint of his teeth, until Adriana writhed against him, the intense sensations somehow arrowing straight to her core.

She explored that glorious torso of his, sun-kissed and hot beneath her hands, her mouth. And all the while she rocked against his hard, proud length, rubbing all of her heat against him helplessly. Wantonly. And he encouraged it, a big hand against the small of her back to hold her against him, keeping her right where he wanted her.

The more she moved the closer he held her, driving her higher and higher, keeping them close but not yet joined, making her whimper with need. Making her die, she thought, over and over and over again.

And then, when she was out of her mind, he kissed her.

Again and again, taking her mouth and making it his, making *her* his, with that devastating mastery that made her feel deliciously weak, made her shake and rock into him and forget her own name. And then at last he was lifting her, arranging her, reaching between them to test her heat with his fingers.

Once. Then again. Then he grinned at her, wicked and knowing, and did something else, a glorious twist of his clever hand—

Adriana shattered around him, a clenching, rolling burst of fire and light.

But Pato wasn't done.

He laughed, she thought, and then the smooth, hot length of him was pressing against her entrance. He wrapped his hands around her hips, held her fast between them, then thrust deep inside.

And she shattered again, instantly, the second explosion building from the first and tearing her into a million brilliant pieces. It went on and on. She gasped and she sobbed and then, when she started to breathe again, he flipped them around on the sofa, so she was lying on her back and he was cradled between her thighs.

"My turn," he whispered, grinning down at her, his eyes lazy and dark, and focused on her as if nothing else existed but this. Her. The two of them together, finally.

At last, Adriana thought.

And then he began to move.

She was exquisite. *Perfect.* Soft and trembling all around him, clinging to him, wild for him, hot cream and soft silk and *his.*

Finally his, and who cared about the consequences.

Pato set a slow, steady pace, watching her as he took her, watching every shimmer of ecstasy, every hint of joy, that crossed her expressive face. Her hips met his with each thrust, moving in a sinuous rhythm that nearly made him lose his mind. And his control.

Slowly, carefully, he built up the fire in her all over again, leaning down to worship her perfect breasts, her lush mouth. He pulled her knees up to cradle his hips, tasted the salt and sweet of her elegant neck. And then, when he couldn't take any more, he reached between them to find the core of her, and pressed there, rocking against her, into her, until she stiffened against him once more.

Then, at last, he let himself go.

And this time, when she shot over the edge he followed her, listening to her scream out his name as they fell.

It's not enough, he thought then, even as he held her to him, their hearts thundering in concert. *It will never be enough.*

And afterward, he let her crawl over him and drive him wild with her sweet kisses, her delighted exploration of his body. He had her again in the shower, losing himself in the heat and the steam and the slick perfection of her skin beneath his hands. He picked her up and pressed her against the glass, her head tipped back and her mouth open in a kind of silent scream as he rode them both straight back into the heart of that shattering fire.

He wouldn't let her dry herself. Succumbing to an urge he chose not to examine, he did it himself, drying every millimeter of her lovely skin with a soft towel, kissing those three distracting freckles below her breasts, then squeezing the water from her hair. He combed through it slowly, holding her captive between his legs as he sat on the bed in the adjoining bedroom. He noted the colors that sifted through his fingers, testing the heavy silk in his hands.

When he was finished he turned her around, and lost himself for a while in the heaven of her lush, hot mouth, its perfect fit against his, that taste of her that flooded into him and made him crazy, and the sheer poetry of her warm, naked curves beneath his hands.

Pato didn't know how he was going to do what he had to do. He shouldn't have indulged himself. He shouldn't have let her distract him. And yet he didn't regret a single moment of it.

Finally, he set her away from him, as hard again as if he'd never had her, and tempted almost past endurance by the soft invitation on her face, the flush he could see everywhere, from her cheeks to the rosy tips of her breasts.

He had never wanted anything more than this woman. He understood he never would.

And then he wrapped her in a cashmere throw

that matched her beautiful eyes, sat her back on the sofa in the living room, where the bed didn't tempt him, and broke the only vow he'd ever made.

"My mother died when I was eighteen," he told her, because he didn't know how else to begin.

Adriana's blond hair was still damp and hung around her face in dark waves, making her look younger than she was. Innocent, despite all the ways he'd touched her, tasted her. He didn't know why that pulled at him, why it made his chest feel tight.

"I know," she said, sitting with her feet tucked beneath her and the cashmere throw wrapped all around her. She looked delicate. *Perfect,* he thought again, and he couldn't have her. Why couldn't he keep that in mind? "I remember."

"Lenz was twenty-five." Pato shoved his hands in the pockets of the jeans he'd yanked back on when they left the bedroom. He roamed the cottage's small living space restlessly as he talked. "He had completed his military service and had taken his place at the king's side. He'd trained his whole life for it, as befits the heir to the throne." Adriana's gaze tracked Pato as he moved, and he smiled slightly. "I was the spare, and had far fewer expectations placed on me. I'd just started university. I paid some attention to my studies, but I was more interested in the girls."

"Shocking," Adriana said drily, but she was smiling.

"I didn't have to be serious," Pato said darkly. "That was Lenz's job. His duty. I always got to be the favorite, the happy disaster, but he was meant to be king."

For a moment, Pato only gazed at her. He'd let her walk out of the palace today thinking he'd turned on her like all the others, like the people who had called her names and made her feel dirty. He'd seen the look on her face, the crushed betrayal she'd tried to hide, and he'd done it anyway.

He couldn't stand it. He couldn't live with it.

And there was only one way to apologize: he had to explain. His life. His choices. Why he couldn't have her no matter how much he wanted her. She'd cried in his arms and he'd meant what he'd said to her, and he didn't have it in him to let her down. Not Adriana. Not this time. The whole world could think he was waste of space, as pointless as he was promiscuous, but he'd found he couldn't handle it if she did, too. He simply couldn't bear it.

"Pato." She was frowning again, deeper this time, and she stood then, the throw draping around her like a cape. "You don't have to tell me anything. You don't have to do this, whatever this is."

"I do," he said, surprised to hear how rough his voice was. "I need you to understand."

He didn't tell her why. He wasn't entirely sure he knew.

She shook her head, smiling slightly. "I don't expect anything from you," she said. "I know who you are and I know who I am. I'm at peace with it."

He blinked, then scowled at her. "What?"

"I love you," she said, so softly he almost thought he'd imagined it. But she was gazing at him, those melting brown eyes warm and glowing, and he knew she'd said it. That she meant it. "And that has nothing to do with what happens here, or after we leave. You don't owe me anything." She held up a hand when he started to talk. "I don't expect or need you to say it back."

Pato stared at her until she grew visibly uncomfortable under the weight of it. Until her sweet expression started to creep back toward a frown.

"The only thing less attractive than watching you attempt to martyr yourself for my brother in my bed," he growled, his temper kicking in as he spoke, like a black band tight around his chest, his gut, "is watching you martyr yourself for me so soon after I've been inside you, listening to you scream out my name." She sucked in an appalled breath, but he didn't stop, couldn't stop, and he stalked toward her until he stood within arm's reach. "I have no desire whatsoever to be quietly and distantly loved by some selfless, bloodless saint locked away in her self-imposed nunnery, prostrating herself daily to whatever it is she thinks she can't have or doesn't deserve. No hairshirt, no mortification of the flesh. No, thank you."

That telltale tide of red swept over her, but this time, he thought, it wasn't so simple as embarrassment. Her eyes narrowed and she drew herself up, pulling the throw tighter around her as if it could protect her from him.

"What an ugly thing to say," she breathed, and he had the impression she was afraid to truly voice the words—as if she thought she might start yelling if she did. He wished she would. "Even for you."

He crossed his arms over his chest and glared at her.

"You want to love me, Adriana?" he demanded,

his voice rough and hot and impatient, welling up from that place inside he'd thought he'd excised long ago, that heart it seemed only she could reach. He'd be damned if he'd let her hide. Not if *he* couldn't. He angled himself closer. "Then love me. Make it hurt. Make it jealous and possessive and painful. Make demands. Make it real or don't bother."

CHAPTER NINE

THERE WERE STAINS of red high on Adriana's cheeks, a dazed look on her pretty face, and Pato gave in to his driving need to be closer to her. Closer, always closer, no matter how irritated he might be with her and her proclamation of so-called love, as tepid as whatever she'd imagined she felt for Lenz.

Pato reached over and sat her down on the sofa, then gripped the back of it, pinning her there with an arm on either side of her. Caging her. Putting his face too close to hers. He couldn't read the way she looked at him then, didn't understand the darkness in her gaze, that sheen that suggested emotions she'd prefer to conceal from him.

"I know all about hiding, Adriana," he said quietly, though he could still hear that edge in his voice. He could feel it inside him. "I can see it when it's right in front of me."

"I don't know why you want to tell me anything."

There was a raggedness in her voice, and he could see it in her face. "I don't know why you hunted me down at the villa, why you brought me here. It would have been easier to simply let me go this morning. Isn't that why you did it?"

"You know why." He wanted to touch her. Taste that lovely mouth. Take her again and again until neither of them could speak. But he didn't. He couldn't. "I can't have you, Adriana, but it's not because I don't want you."

She didn't say a word, but she was breathing high and hard, as if climbing a steep hill. He could see that same darkness in her eyes, deeper now. Her confusion. He pushed away from the sofa but continued to stand over her, looking down at this woman who might, in fact, be the death of him. She'd already ruined him; that much was certain.

"My mother left behind some personal papers," he said then. It was time to finish this, before he forgot why he wanted that, too. "She left them to my father, which seemed an odd choice, given his profound disinterest in her personal affairs while she was alive. But eventually, he read them. And discovered that Lenz was not, in fact, his biological son."

It was Pato's greatest secret, it wasn't only *his* secret, and she could use it to topple his brother's kingdom if she chose. And there it lay, huge and ugly between them, taking up all the air in the cottage.

Adriana made a small, shocked noise, and covered her mouth with her hands. Pato let her simply stare at him, let all the implications sink in. For long moments she seemed frozen. But eventually, she blinked.

"Did Lenz know?" she asked in a whisper.

"We were both called before the king." Pato could hear the grimness in his voice. He'd never told this story before—he'd never imagined he would tell it to anyone. It certainly wasn't part of the plan. "He informed us that a great crime had been perpetrated against the throne of Kitzinia, and that it must be rectified. That was how Lenz found out."

Adriana's eyes closed, as if that was too horrible to imagine. Pato had been there, and he felt much the same. He and Lenz had been ordered before the king, commanded to appear, even though Pato had been in England and Lenz in South Africa at the time. Pato remembered how baffled they'd been, jet-lagged and even somewhat concerned about their father. Until the nasty, furious way he had delivered the news, as if Lenz had engineered his paternity himself for the sole purpose of deception.

"You have no brother from this day forward," the king had intoned into the stunned, sick silence, glaring at Pato as if Lenz had disappeared into thin air. "You are my heir, and your mother's bastard is nothing to you."

"But," Pato had begun, his head spinning. "Father—"

"I have one son," the king had snarled. "One heir to this throne, Patricio, and God have mercy on this kingdom, but it's you."

Pato had never cared much for his father before that day. He'd always been a distant, disapproving presence who had rarely lowered himself to interact much with his second son, which had always suited Pato well enough, as he'd seen what it was like for Lenz to have all that critical attention focused on him. But after that day, Pato had loathed him.

"My father cannot bear scandal," he said now. "He is obsessed with even the slightest speck of dirt anywhere near his spotless reputation. And I had recently landed myself in the tabloids for the first time with an extremely inappropriate British pop star. The king was not pleased about it when I was merely the ornamental second son, or so I heard through the usual channels, but when it turned out I was his heir, he went apoplectic."

Adriana was still sitting there, so straight and shocked, her eyes still wide. "Did he plan to simply toss Lenz out on the street?"

"He did." Pato moved to the nearby armchair and lowered himself into it. "He thought he'd wait until my pop star scandal faded, exile Lenz from Kitzinia and force me to take on the duties of a crown prince in a sober and serious manner that would indicate my brush with the tabloids was no more than a regrettable, youthful indiscretion, never to be repeated."

Adriana only stared at him, shaking her head slightly as if she couldn't take it in. Or perhaps she was attempting to imagine him in the role of dutiful crown prince—a stretch for anyone, he was well aware. Even him.

"Lenz's exile was to be presented as an abdication well before he was to take the throne." Pato smiled slightly. Darkly. "But I never let the scandal die down. From that day forward, I made it my job to be an embarrassment. To make it abundantly clear that I was and am unfit for any kind of throne."

"Pato." She shifted then, moving forward in her seat as if she wanted to reach over and touch him. Her hands moved, but then she held them together in her lap. "You know I admire your brother. But if you're the heir to the throne…?" She searched his face. "Isn't it your birthright?"

"You sound like Lenz," Pato said roughly. He had to get up again then, had to move, and found himself staring out the windows that looked down to the peaceful water. "I never envied Lenz his position. I never wished for his responsibilities. And when they were handed to me, I didn't want them. Can you imagine if it was announced I was supposed to be king? The people would take up arms and riot in the streets."

"They might object to the Playboy Prince, yes," Adriana said after a long moment. "You've made sure of that. But that's not who you are."

His breath left him. He ignored the ache in his chest.

"My choice was a throne or a brother," he said

quietly. He turned to face her. "I chose my brother. And I don't regret it."

"Pato…" she whispered, and the look in her eyes nearly undid him.

"Since then," he said gruffly, pushing forward because he couldn't stay in this moment, couldn't let himself explore the way she gazed at him, "my father has had to pretend to keep Lenz in his good graces, because his pride won't allow him to explain the situation to his ministers. Especially when, as you say, I've made certain the alternative is so unacceptable."

For a moment there was nothing in the room but the sound of his own pounding heart.

"You're a good man, Pato," Adriana said then. There was a scratchy undertone to her voice that made him think she was holding back tears. For him. And he thought it might undo him. "And a very good brother."

Pato looked at her, then away, before he forgot what he could and couldn't have. Before he forgot he'd chosen to be a hollow man, with an empty life. Before he was tempted to believe her.

"My father is also unwell," he said instead, bitterly. "It is, ironically enough, his heart."

* * *

Adriana was worried about her own.

She hardly knew where to look, what to think. Nothing he was telling her could possibly be true—and yet it all made a horrible sense. It explained the chilliness she'd always sensed between Lenz and the king. It explained Lenz's extraordinary patience with Pato's messy escapades. More, it explained how Pato could do all the scandalous things he'd done and yet also be the man who'd held her on the plane, then quietly rid her of a lifetime of shame. It explained everything.

He stood there at the window so calmly, half-naked as ever, all sun-kissed skin and masculine grace, talking with such seeming nonchalance about things that would overthrow their government. He had given up a throne. He loved his brother more than he wanted what was his by birthright. He had deliberately crafted his own mythology to serve his own ends and to force his father, the king, into doing what he wanted him to do. He'd even hinted at this once before, in London, when he'd said his reputation was his life's work.

He was truly remarkable, she thought then. And he was hers.

It didn't matter for how long. It didn't matter if he couldn't have her, as he'd said. It didn't matter if all she ever had of him was the distance and the unrequited love that he'd mocked. He'd given her his secrets. He'd stepped out of hiding and shown her who he really was, because he believed she deserved to know. Because he hadn't wanted to let her leave him the way she had this morning, thinking the worst of him.

He would rather have her know the dangerous truth than have her think he didn't care.

That he cared, that he must or he would never have shared any of this with her, that he really must trust her, dawned inside her like the sun.

He was hers.

"His health is deteriorating, he is not a candidate for surgery and he is an unacceptable risk to the kingdom," Pato was saying. "He should have stepped down already. He will have no choice when Lenz marries Lissette, as she was betrothed at birth to the heir to the Kitzinian throne." Pato shrugged at Adriana's quizzical look. "If Lenz marries her, it is an assertion that he is, in fact, that heir. There can be no going back unless my father wants an international incident that could well become a war. He will have no choice but to face the inevitable." Pato's mouth moved into a curve that was far darker than usual. "He has grown more desperate by the day for another option."

"You," Adriana said.

"Me," Pato agreed, "even though I've gone to great lengths to keep myself out of the running." He sighed, and then leveled a look at her that made something twist in her stomach, made a sense of foreboding trickle down her back. "He had convinced himself that the kingdom would excuse me as a young man sowing his oats, who could in time settle down, as men do. But now he believes I am skulking about with one of Lenz's cast-off mistresses, which he finds truly distasteful. Worse, he is superstitious enough to believe that Righetti women possess some kind of witchcraft, and that I am weak enough to be under your spell."

Adriana couldn't breathe, as if he'd slammed that straight into her gut. But she couldn't look away from him, either.

"Bewitched by a woman descended from traitors and temptresses," Pato said softly, his golden eyes darker, more intense. "Crafted by the ages to be my downfall."

"You want him to think that," she managed to say, despite feeling as if the room were drawing tight on all sides. "That's why you decided to behave these last weeks. You wanted him to think I was influencing you."

"Yes."

His gaze was dark. Demanding. Without apology, and Adriana felt so brittle, suddenly. So close to breaking, and that wave of misery she'd thought she was rid of waited there for her, she knew. In the next breath. Or the one following. And it would crash over her and take her to her knees if she let it.

But she still couldn't look away from him.

"Was it all a game?" she whispered, that familiar emptiness opening again inside her, reminding her how easy it was to be sucked back in. "Was any of it real?"

"You know that it was both." His gaze bored into her, challenging her. "Almost from the very beginning."

She shook her head, aware that it felt too full, too fragile. That she did. There was too much noise in her ears and that dark pit in her stomach, and all she wanted was to get to her feet and run—but she couldn't seem to move.

"I don't know that."

"You do."

He pushed away from the wall and came toward her then, imposing and beautiful, and she knew the truth about him now. She knew his indolence was an act, that the powerful, ruthless man she'd glimpsed was who Pato was. Now she couldn't pretend she didn't see it. She couldn't pretend he was lazy, pointless, careless—any of the things he'd pretended he was. He'd manipulated her every step of the way and would no doubt do it again. He'd given up a throne for this. What was one woman next to that? She was nothing but collateral damage.

And still, she didn't move. Still, her heart ached for him. No matter what this meant for her, what it said about the last years of her life.

"This is why you have to leave the palace, Adriana," he said, that dark urgency in his voice and stamped across his face. "You deserve better than these games. No one comes out of them without being compromised. No one wins."

She struggled with the tears that pricked suddenly at the back of her eyes, and then he was right there, sinking down in front of her to kneel on the floor and take her face between his hands.

"I don't want to let you go," he whispered fiercely. "But I will. Somehow, I will. I promise."

The same old voices snaked through her then, crawling out of that darkness inside her to whisper the same old poison. *He wanted the Righetti whore and he got her, didn't he?* She'd been a means to an end for him, a tool. *Another instrument.* Something he could use and then toss aside. *"Remember who you are, Adriana,"* her father had said when she'd first got the job at the palace. *"Remember that your disgrace is already assumed—they only seek confirmation."* She was nothing but her surname, her face, her family's everlasting shame, another headline in another tabloid paper. Temptresses and a traitor, marking her as surely as if she wore their sins tattooed across her cheeks.

But Pato had trusted her. He'd come for her when he could have simply let her leave, none the wiser. He'd brought her here, and she'd been the one to insist they give in to the wild passion between them, not Pato. He'd wanted to talk and she hadn't let him. And now he'd told her everything, and yes, it hurt. But he'd told her a story that could rock the whole kingdom, and he wanted to set her free. Again.

And all *she* wanted to do, all she could think to do, was run away and hide—which was just what she'd done when she was seventeen. It was what she always did.

No wonder he'd mocked her declaration of love, she thought then, a different kind of shame winding through her. It wasn't love at all. It was safe and removed. It was loving the idea of him, not loving the man. The complicated, dangerous man, who wasn't safe at all and had never pretended otherwise—he only made her feel that she might be safe when she was with him.

Make it hurt, he'd challenged her, scowling at her, refusing to accept her half measures. *Make it real or don't bother.*

And this was her chance to step out of hiding, just as he'd done. She wanted to be bold. She wanted to feel *alive.* For once in her life, she wanted to use her infamous name and her notoriety instead of sitting back and letting others use it against her.

Not as a sacrifice. Pato deserved better than that. He deserved a gift.

"It sounds like I'm an excellent weapon," she said. She wrapped her hands around his wrists, tilted her face to his and lost herself in all that dark gold. "Why don't you use me? I'm sure your father isn't the only one who assumes that I'm your mistress as well as Lenz's. Why not make it public and damn yourself in his eyes forever?"

"I'm not going to use you that way, Adriana." Pato's voice was harsh. "I didn't accept the offer when it was for Lenz, and I won't do it now. You are not a whore. You do not wield dark magic that turns unsuspecting men into your slaves. You're better than this fairy-tale villain they've made you, that I've helped them make you, and I refuse to take part in it any longer. I won't."

She couldn't help herself then. She leaned in and kissed him, feeling the electric charge that shuddered through him, then sizzled in her, making what she'd intended to be sweet turn into something else entirely. When she pulled away, his eyes were still dark, but gleamed gold.

"I'm genetically predisposed to be the mistress of a Kitzinian prince," she told him, and smiled at him. She could do this. In truth, she already had.

"And I'm already notorious. You may not want to accept your birthright, Pato, but I do."

He looked at her for what felt like a very long time. His hands still cupped her cheeks, and she was sure he could see through her, all the way down to the deepest part of her soul.

"I won't let you sacrifice yourself for this kingdom," he said finally, his gaze more gold than grim, though his mouth remained serious. "It has never done anything for you but make your life a misery."

"It's no sacrifice," she said, her hands tightening around his wrists. "I don't want to martyr myself, I want to help."

Another long moment, taut and electric, and then he shook his head.

"We have a week until the wedding." Pato stood, drawing her to her feet and into his arms. As he gazed down at her, his mouth began to curve into that wicked quirk she recognized. "Lenz will marry his ice princess, the poor bastard. The spectacle will bring in hordes of tourists, just as my parents' wedding did a generation ago. My father will finally cede the throne, and will spend the rest of his miserable life faced with the knowledge that the son he raised and then rejected is his king. And life will carry on, Adriana, without a single mention of the Righetti family, traitors and tempt-resses, or you."

"But—"

"I promise," he whispered against her mouth.

And then he kissed her, igniting fire and need and that searing joy, and she decided there were far better things to do with the man she loved than argue.

For now.

Adriana woke the morning before the royal wedding with a smile on her face. She turned off her alarm and settled back against her pillow, smiling at the light pouring in through her windows as if the sun shone only for her. As if it was simply another gift Pato had given her.

They hadn't spoken again of his letting her go.

Pato was not considered a legendary lover by accident, she'd learned. His reputed skills were no tabloid exaggeration. He'd had her twice more before they'd left the cottage that day, reducing her to a sobbing, writhing mess again and again, until she was deliciously limp, content simply to cling to him on the drive back into the city, thinking not of thrones and notoriety but him. Only him.

"Come to the palace tomorrow," he'd told her, letting her off on a deserted corner some distance from her family's villa, out of the circle of light thrown by the nearest streetlamp, safe from prying eyes and gossiping tongues.

"You sacked me," she'd reminded him primly. He'd grinned at her, sitting on that lethal-looking motorcycle and holding fast to one of her hands.

"I changed my mind. I do that." His wicked brows rose. "It is my great royal privilege."

"I'm not sure I want the job," she'd teased. "My employer is embarrassing and often inappropriately dressed. And the hours are terrible."

He'd tugged her to him then, kissing her as slowly and as thoroughly as if he hadn't done so already that day, too many times to count. He kissed her until she was boneless against him, and only then did he let her go.

"Don't be late," he'd said, his eyes gleaming in the dark. "And I do hope you can behave yourself. I can't have my assistant throwing herself at me at every opportunity. I take my position as the royal ornament and national disaster very seriously."

He'd roared off, splitting the night with the noise his motorcycle made, and Adriana had fairly danced all the way back to the villa.

And then, the following morning, he'd sauntered into his office wearing nothing but a pair of dark trousers low on his narrow hips. He'd shut the door behind him and had her over his desk before he'd even said good-morning. She'd had to bite her own hand to make sure she stayed quiet while Pato moved inside her, whispering dark and thrilling things in her ear, pushing them both straight over the edge.

He'd started as he meant to go on, Adriana thought now, rolling out of her bed and padding into her bath. They'd followed his usual schedule, packed this week with extra wedding requirements. The difference was, every time they were alone they'd been unable to keep their hands off each other. The car, his office, even a blazingly hot encounter all of three steps away from a corporate luncheon. He'd simply glanced into what was probably a coatroom, pulled her inside and braced her against a chair that sat near the far wall.

"Hang on," he'd murmured, leaning over her back and wrapping his hands around her hips. And then he'd thrust into her, hot and hard and devastatingly talented, and she'd stopped caring about the speech he'd been meant to give. She'd cared about nothing at all but the wild blaze between them and the way they both burned in it, together.

Adriana left her bedroom then, twisting her hair up into a knot as she walked through the villa in search of her morning coffee. She felt lighter than she had in years. She smiled down the hallways toward that closed-off parlor, and took her time descending the grand stairs.

Last night Pato had been called upon to entertain visiting dignitaries and royals from across Europe, all in town for the wedding. When the long evening was over and they were alone in his car, he'd pulled Adriana to him. He'd tucked her beneath his arm, arranged her legs over his lap and rested his chin on the top of her head. Then he'd simply held her. When his driver started up the hill toward the Righetti villa, he'd hit the intercom and told him to simply keep driving.

They'd driven for a long time, circling around and around the city. Pato had played with her hair idly. She'd closed her eyes and let herself enjoy the luxury of time to bask in him. He'd held her close against his heart while the city bled light and noise all around them.

Inside the car, it had been quiet. Soft. Perfect. And Adriana had never felt more cherished. More loved.

She didn't notice the strained silence in the kitchen until she was pouring herself a cup of coffee. She turned to find her father staring at her, an arrested expression on his face she'd never seen before. Even her mother looked pale, one hand clutching at her heart as if it were broken, her eyes cast down toward the table.

"What's happened?" Adriana asked, terrified. She left her coffee on the counter and took a step toward the table, looking back and forth between her parents. Was it one of her brothers? "Has there been an accident?"

Her mother only shook her head as if she couldn't bear to speak, squeezing her eyes shut, and Adriana went cold.

"You know what you've done," her father stated in a hard voice. "And now, Adriana, so does the world."

It took her a moment to understand what he was saying—and that he really was speaking to her with all that chilly animosity. And when she did understand it, she shook her head in confusion.

"I don't know what you mean," she said.

"I blame myself." Her father pushed back his chair and climbed to his feet, looking far older than he had the day before. Adriana felt a deep pang of fear. Then he stood there for a moment, his hard gaze raking over her as if she was something dirty.

And she knew, then.

That familiar, panicked cold bloomed deep inside her, spreading out and turning black, ripping open that same old wound and letting the emptiness back in.

He knew about Pato.

"Papa," she said softly, reaching out a hand toward him, but he recoiled. Her throat constricted when she tried to swallow, and she slowly dropped her arm back to her side.

"I knew you were too beautiful," he told her in that terrible voice, and Adriana felt it like a knife, sinking deep into her belly. "I knew it would ruin us. Beauty like that is only the surface, Adriana, and everything beneath it is corrupt. Sinful. Twisted. I saw it myself in Sandrine, in her contempt for propriety. It runs in this family like a disease. I knew it was in you since the day you were born a girl."

She felt unsteady on her feet, as if he'd actually cut her open. Perhaps it would have been better—less painful—if he had. And she was too aware of her mother's continued silence in place of her usual unspoken support, weighing on Adriana like an indictment.

"There's no Righetti family disease," she said when she could speak. It was hard to keep her voice calm, her gaze steady as she faced her father. "There never was. We're only people, Papa, and we all make our own choices."

His lip curled, and he stared at her as if he'd never seen her before now. As if she'd worn a mask her whole life, until today, and what he saw beneath it disgusted him. It made her feel sick.

"Tell me he forced you. Coerced you. Tell me, daughter, that you did not betray your family's trust in you willingly. That you did not follow in the footsteps of all the whores who sullied the Righetti name before you and take *Prince Pato*—" he spat out the name as if it was the foulest of curses "—as your lover. Tell me you are not so stupid as to open your legs for that degenerate. *Tell me*."

Adriana didn't understand how this was happening. Her head pounded and her heart felt like lead in her chest, and she didn't know what to do, how to make this better. How to explain what it was like to be free of her chains to the man who'd helped fashion them, because he wore so many of his own.

"He's not a degenerate," she whispered, and it was a mistake.

Her father let out a kind of roar—enraged and humiliated and broken. It made her mother jerk in her chair. It made Adriana want to cry. But instead, she wrapped her arms around her middle and watched him, waiting for his eyes to meet hers again.

When they did, she thought the look in them might leave marks.

"You don't understand," she said quickly, desperately.

"I cannot bear to look at you." He sounded deeply, irreversibly disgusted. It made her eyes fill with tears. "All I see are his fingerprints, sullying you. Ruining you. Making you nothing more than one more Righetti whore, like all the rest." He shook his head. "You have proved to the world that we are tainted. Dirty. You have destroyed us all over again, Adriana, and for what? The chance to be one more conquest in an endless line? The opportunity to warm a bed that has never gone cold? How could you?"

She shook, but she didn't move, not even when he turned and slammed out of the room, the silence he left behind heavy and loud, pressing into her, making her want to slide into a ball on the floor. But she didn't do it. She forced herself to look at her mother instead.

"Mama—" she began, but her mother shook her head hard, her lips pressed together in a tight line.

"You knew better," she said in a harsh whisper. "From the time you were small, you knew better than this. Righettis can't put a single foot wrong. Righettis must be above reproach—especially a girl who looks like you, as if you stepped out of one of those paintings. I took you to meet Sandrine myself—living out her days in a foreign country with a man who should have been a duke, cast out from her home forever. *You knew better.*"

It was such an unexpected slap that Adriana took a step back from the table, as if her mother really had hit her.

"I never did anything to be ashamed of," she blurted out, something reckless moving in her then, impossible to contain, as if she'd waited all her life for this conversation. "And yet the first thing you taught me was shame. Why do we punish ourselves before anyone else does?" Her voice cracked. "Why did you?"

But that made it worse. Her mother stood then, straight and sorrowful, both hands at her heart and her eyes like nails, staring at Adriana as if she was a stranger.

"You've made your bed, Adriana," she said coldly. "We'll all have to lie in it, won't we? I certainly hope it was worth it. Sandrine always thought so, but then, she died alone and far away, in a cloud of disgrace. And so will you."

Her mother didn't slam the door when she left. She simply walked away and didn't look back, which was worse. Worse than a slap.

And Adriana stood there in all that silence, awful and simmering and ugly, and tried to keep herself from falling apart.

She looked around desperately, as if a solution might rise up from the tiled floor, and that was when she saw the paper spread out in the middle of the wooden table as if her parents had pored over it together.

The paper.

For a moment she couldn't bring herself to look, because she could imagine what she'd see. She'd been imagining it, in one form or another, since she was a girl. She'd had nightmares about it more than once. She stared at the paper as if it were a serpent coiled up in the middle of the kitchen, fangs extended.

But in the end, she couldn't help herself.

Playboy Pato Succumbs to Witchy Righetti's Spell! Well known for her notorious wiles, Adriana Righetti—very much an heir to her family's storied charms—has made a shocking play for the kingdom's favorite bachelor—

She couldn't do it, she told herself, squeezing her eyes shut, her hand at her throat as if her pulse might leap out from beneath her skin.

But there was more. She had to look.

There was the helpful sidebar that ran down all the infamous members of the Righetti family, complete with pictures and a few snide lines detailing their sins. Carolina, shameless mistress to Crown Prince and later King Philip. Maria, rumored to have slept with all three royal princes and some assorted cousins with dukedoms in an effort to trade upward, until she reached Eduardo, the future king. Francesca, lifelong consort of Prince Vidal. Sandrine, who'd disrupted the Reinsmark dukedom. And Almado the traitor, who had assassinated King Oktav. And somehow it managed to suggest, without ever doing so directly, that Adriana herself had been mistress to all those Kitzinian royals before going on to personally betray the country, before taking her position in the palace and turning her attention to the easily seduced and obviously beguiled Pato.

And then there were the pictures.

They'd been taken the day before yesterday, she saw at once. She reached out to run a shaky finger over the series of photos before her, smudging the newspaper ink. She'd thought they were alone. Pato had spent the morning at an event, and they had been waiting in the antechamber of the hall for his driver to pull around. She'd been *certain* they were alone.

And that was why she hadn't protested when

he'd turned to her with that wild and hungry look in his eyes. Why she'd leaned into him when he'd taken her mouth in a lush promise of a kiss. It had been devastating and quick, a mere appetizer to what he'd do once they climbed into the car, he'd informed her with that gleam of gold in his eyes. And he'd kept his word.

It had been a single kiss. Hot and private. *Theirs.*

But the pictures looked openly carnal. The very number of photographs made it seem they'd kissed for a long time, so focused on each other that they were reckless, careless. The paper tutted about the locale and the fact that neither of them had apparently noticed or cared that they'd been in public—"par for the course for Pato, but can Adriana's history make her anything but a terrible influence on the kingdom's bad boy?"

She had no idea how long she stood there in the kitchen, all alone with the newspaper and its malicious recounting and reshaping of her life into nasty little innuendos and silly nicknames. At first she didn't know what snapped her out of it—but then she heard the banging at the door, harsh and loud. And the shouting.

Her stomach sank to her feet. Paparazzi.

She should have expected them. She'd dealt with them a thousand times before—but never when *she* was the target. Adriana took a deep breath, and then pulled all the curtains shut without letting them get a glimpse of her, took the landline telephone off its hook, making it as difficult as possible for the cockroaches swarming in her street to get what they were after.

She didn't seek out her parents. They would expect an apology—an apology Adriana doubted they would accept. And she might feel sick to her stomach, she might feel battered and attacked, exposed and alone, but she wasn't sorry.

When she finally climbed back up to her room, her mobile was lit up with messages. Reporters. Supposed "friends" she hadn't spoken to in years. Her few actual friends, quietly wondering how she was. More reporters. And then the clipped and frigid tones of the king's private secretary, a man Adriana had seen from afar but had certainly never met, informing her that her services to the royal household were no longer required.

She was cut off. Dismissed. The Righetti contamination had been officially removed from the palace.

It was not until dusk began to creep through the streets that Adriana admitted to herself that she'd expected Pato to appear again—to race to the villa and save her, somehow, from this public disgrace. Make it better, even if this public stoning via newspaper was exactly what she'd volunteered for. Twice.

Because it turned out that being called a whore her whole life had not, in fact, prepared her for what it was like to see it printed in the newspapers and all across the internet, not as speculation this time, but fact. It hadn't prepared her for that scene in the kitchen with her parents. It hadn't prepared her at all.

And when she'd wanted to do this, she understood as she sat there, barricaded in her childhood bedroom, she'd thought only about how Lenz or Pato might benefit from this kind of media attention. She hadn't thought about her family at all, and the guilt of that grew heavier as the day wore on. This wasn't only about her. It never had been. This was her family's nightmare, and she'd made it real.

Pato had been right. She'd been so busy rushing to martyr herself that she hadn't stopped to consider precisely what that might entail. Or just how many people it would hurt besides her.

Eventually, she had to accept the fact that Pato wasn't coming.

And with it, a wave of other things she didn't want to think about. Such as how ruthless he really was, how manipulative. He'd told her so himself. How he'd promised this wouldn't happen, and yet it had. And what his silence today suggested that meant.

She couldn't cry. She could hardly move. It simply hurt too much.

Late that night, Adriana found herself in the parlor with the other harlots. She curled up in the chair below their portraits and stared at them until her eyes went blurry.

This was inevitable from the start, she told herself. *You walked right into it anyway, talking about love and imagining you were better than your past.*

Adriana had no one to blame for this but herself.

CHAPTER TEN

ADRIANA WOKE WITH a start, her heart pounding.

For a moment she didn't know where she was, but even as she uncurled herself from the chair she found herself in, she remembered, and a glance at the wall before her, and the three portraits hanging there, confirmed it.

Adriana stretched out the kink in her neck, the events of the previous day flooding back to her, one after the next, as she stood. Her father's face. Her mother's harsh words. The newspapers, the paparazzi. Pato's obvious betrayal. She shut her eyes against it, as if that might make it all vanish.

Last night she hadn't been able to cry. This morning, she refused to let herself indulge the urge. If the women hanging on the wall could smile, she told herself, then so could she.

She squared her shoulders, told herself she was ready to face the next battle—and that was when she heard the shouting. *Her father.*

Adriana threw open the door and stepped into the hall, moving toward the angry sound. Her stomach twisted into a hard knot as she tried to imagine what could be worse than yesterday's newspaper spread, which hadn't sent him into this kind of temper—

"You've done enough damage—you can want nothing more! Will you take the house down, brick by brick? Demand our blood from the stones?" Her father sounded upset and furious in a way that scared her, it was so much worse than yesterday. She picked up her speed. "How many of your sick, twisted little games—"

Adriana reached the stair, looked down and froze solid.

Pato stood there in the lower hall.

She didn't know what poured through her then, so intense it was like an acute flash of pain, and she couldn't tear her eyes away from him.

Pato wore the ceremonial military regalia that tradition dictated served as formal wear to a grand state occasion like his brother's wedding, a dark navy uniform accented in deep scarlet at the cuffs, the neck, and in lines down each leg, then liberally adorned with golden epaulets and brocades that trumpeted his rank. He'd even tamed his hair from its usual wildness, making him look utterly, heartbreakingly respectable. He stood tall and forbidding, staring at Adriana's father impassively, a trio of guards arranged behind him.

He looked every inch the royal prince he was. Like the king he could have been. He looked dangerously beautiful and completely inaccessible, and it ripped at her heart.

Adriana sucked in a breath, and his gaze snapped to hers, finding her there on the landing.

His gaze was the darkest she'd ever seen it, hard and intense, and she didn't know how long they stood there, eyes locked together. Her father was blocking the stairs, his voice louder by the second, and yet while Pato looked at her like that, she hardly heard him.

Pato jerked his gaze away abruptly, leaving Adriana feeling simultaneously relieved and bereft.

"No more," he said curtly, cutting into her father's diatribe with a tone of sheer command. He seemed taller, more formidable, and yet he didn't change expression as he stared at her father. "You forget yourself."

The air in the villa went taut. Thin. Adriana's father fell silent. Pato waited.

One breath. Another.

"Step aside," Pato ordered, his voice even, but there was no mistaking the crack of power in it. The expectation of obedience. The guards behind him stood straighter. "I won't ask again."

Adriana's father moved out of his way, and even as he did, Pato brushed past him, taking the steps with a controlled ferocity that made something inside Adriana turn over and start to heat. She couldn't seem to look away from him as he bore down on her, or even catch her breath, and then he was there. Prince Patricio of Kitzinia, in all his stately splendor, looking at her with the same hard intensity as before, nothing the least bit gold in his gaze.

"You brought guards?" she asked. Of all the things she might have said to him.

"I dislike the paparazzi blocking my movements," he said in that same even tone. Then his head tilted slightly. Regally. "Is there a private room?"

It was another command, demanding instant compliance.

Adriana didn't hesitate any more than her father had. She waved her hand down the hall she'd come from, and Pato inclined his head, indicating she should precede him.

She did—but not without looking back.

Her father stood in the lower hall, watching her with the same tortured expression he'd worn yesterday, and the guilt swept through her again, almost choking her. She opened her mouth, as if there was something she could say to take away his horror at what was his worst nightmare come to life, right before his eyes.

But Pato's hand was on the small of her back, urging her ahead of him. There was nothing she could say to make this better. Her father wouldn't forgive her, and on some level, she didn't blame him. She'd known better than to do this, and she'd done it anyway.

Adriana couldn't stand Pato touching her—it was too much to bear, and her body only wanted him the way it always did—so she broke away as she led him back into the parlor, moving all the way across the room before facing him, her back to the far wall.

Pato stepped inside, closed the door behind him,

and his gaze cut immediately to the trio of paintings on the wall. He went still, his mouth flattening into a grim line.

It took him a long time to look at her again, but when he did, Adriana had recovered herself. Maybe it was the women on the wall, reminding her that she could do this, whatever this was. It took a lot of strength to survive being as hated as they'd been—as she was. She remembered that Sandrine's eyes had sparkled merrily when she'd met her, that the older woman had looked anything but cowed.

Adriana could survive these final, painful scenes with Pato. *She could.*

"I would have preferred to sacrifice myself, I think," she said coolly, pulling the familiar defense around her gratefully. She crossed her arms and ignored that flash in his gaze. "Rather than wake up yesterday to find myself burned to a crisp on your little pyre with no warning whatsoever. Call me controlling if you must."

He eyed her from across the room in a way that unnerved her, but she refused to back down.

"You believe I did this?" he asked mildly. But she knew him too well to be fooled by that tone.

"I don't know why you didn't ask for assistance," she continued, as if this was any other conversation she'd ever had with him. As if it was easy to pretend there was no emotion beneath this, no dark whirling thing that threatened to suck her under. "I've been handling your paparazzi encounters for a long time, Pato. At the very least, I might have suggested a better nickname for myself than 'Witchy Righetti.'"

Again, he gave her a long look, and it occurred to her belatedly that he was fighting for calm and control as much as she was. It made her heart kick in a kind of panic.

"I promised you I wouldn't use you that way," he reminded her, almost politely. As if he thought she might have forgotten.

And it was too much. He was here, and the way he was dressed made the difference in their situations painfully clear to her. He would walk away from this a prince. She would crawl away from this the disgraced daughter of a despised family, personally responsible for this new helping of shame and recrimination heaped on her family's name.

She used the only weapon she had.

"You also promised your brother that you

wouldn't reveal his secret, I assume," she said, very distinctly, and told herself she was pleased when she saw something dark and raw in his gaze. "And yet you did. Why would I think you'd keep a relatively small promise to someone like me?"

A muscle worked in his jaw. His hands curled into fists. And he looked at her as if she'd torn him wide-open.

Adriana told herself she was glad. He wasn't here to save her. He couldn't undo what she'd done to her family. But if she could make him feel a little bit of what she did, all the better—even if that look on his face clawed into her, shredding her from within.

He laughed, but it was short. Bitter.

"This, then, is what you mean when you say you love me," he said quietly, his dark eyes pinning her to the wall behind her. "Is it better this way, Adriana? If you succeed in running me off—if you take that knife and bury it deep enough, twist it hard enough—will that get you what you want?"

He was moving toward her—one step, then another—dark and furious and something more than that. Something that made him look as destroyed as she felt, and there was nothing good about that at all.

"I don't want—" she began, but he laughed again, and this time, it made her shudder.

"I think you do," he said, low and intense. Damning her where she stood. "I think you want to hole up in this mausoleum and paint your own portrait to hang on that wall." He pointed at the trinity of pictures, but he didn't take his eyes off her. "That's what Righettis have been doing in this place for the last hundred years, wafting through the kingdom like ghosts, subjecting themselves to whatever punishment is thrown their way—"

"You don't have any idea what you're talking about!" she cried, aware that she was shouting. But there was something hard and itchy and hot inside her, and she had to get it out or it would kill her, she knew. "It's not as if you have any idea what it's like to be the most reviled family in the kingdom. And why would you? It wasn't *your* ancestor who murdered the king!" She swept her hand toward the portraits. "Or slept with several branches of the royal family tree!"

His eyes blazed at her, and she realized only belatedly that he'd come much too close to her, as if he'd stalked her without her noticing.

"Do you imagine that my family took control of the throne of Kitzinia because we asked nicely?" he demanded, sounding as incredulous as he did angry. "Is that how you remember the history of Europe? Because to my recollection, every kingdom that ever was came about in blood and treachery." He shook his head, and then somehow his hands were on her upper arms and he was even closer, and she knew she should push him away. She knew she should extricate herself—but she couldn't seem to move. "Your family isn't the only one in the kingdom with blood on its hands, Adriana. But it is certainly the only one I can think of that's created a cult out of its guilt!"

She hung there, unable to breathe, unable to think, suspended between his hands as surely as she was caught in that dark, ferocious glare he kept trained on her.

"What do mean by that?" she asked in a whisper, and then shivered when he pulled her so close to him that his lips almost touched her as he spoke.

"You didn't kill any Kitzinian kings," he snapped. "And last I checked, the only prince you've slept with is me. Stop accepting the blame for history you can't change." Something flashed in his gaze then, and she felt the echo deep inside her, deep and threatening, as if might tear her in two. "For God's sake," he growled at her. "*You* are not a painting on the wall, Adriana. You don't have to shoulder this. *Fight back*."

Pato let go of her and stepped away.

He couldn't remember the last time he'd lost his temper. Not like this, so that it hummed in him still. And certainly not with that rough edge of need running through it, making him want nothing more than to continue this conversation while naked and deep inside her.

Even after she'd thrown what he'd told her in his face, he wanted her, with the same desperation as before. More, perhaps. He didn't know whether to laugh at that or simply despair of himself.

Adriana was breathing hard, and looking very little like the brazen harlot he'd read so much about yesterday. He could see the smudges of exhaustion beneath her beautiful eyes, the vulnerable cast to her sweet mouth, the flush in her cheeks that failed to disguise the paleness of her face. He let his gaze fall over her, from the blond waves in a messy knot on the back of her head, to a face scrubbed free of cosmetics, to the loose cotton clothes she wore that might very well be her pajamas. And her bare feet.

For some reason, the fact that he could see her toes made his chest hurt.

"I didn't plant that story," he told her then, biting out the words he shouldn't have to say. She raised a hand to her mouth as if she thought she might cry, then lowered it again, as if she was still trying to put on a front for him. He hated it. "It was Lissette."

"What?" Adriana shook her head. "Why?"

"Lenz told her the truth." Adriana's eyes flew to his, shocked. "He felt she deserved to make an informed decision about whether or not to marry him. She, in turn, felt that my father couldn't be trusted not to pull a last-minute stunt at the wedding, so she decided to make it clear that he was without options."

Adriana swallowed. "Lenz must be happy that she wants him anyway."

"That, or she very much wants to be queen of Kitzinia," Pato retorted. His voice lowered. "But I'm certainly pleased to learn that your opinion of me is as poor today as it ever was. And why is that, do you suppose?"

She blinked, and when she looked at him again, there was an anguish in her eyes that tore at him.

"You've been working toward this for a very long time," she said in a hushed tone. "You've given up so much. I thought that if you needed to do it, you would. And I'd volunteered, hadn't I?" He only watched her, until she shifted uncomfortably, her expression pure misery. "It seemed like the kind of thing you'd do."

"Why?" he asked quietly, though his voice was like a blade. He could see it cut at her. "What makes me so untrustworthy, Adriana?"

"I never said that," she whispered, but she was trembling.

"I know why," he told her. "And so do you. At the end of the day, I'm nothing more than a whore myself, and in my case, a real one. And who could possibly trust a whore?"

She flinched, and then she simply collapsed. Her hands flew up to cover her face and she bent over her knees, and for a simmering moment, Pato thought she was sick. But then he saw the sobs shake her body, silent and racking.

Pato couldn't stay away from her, not when she was falling apart right in front of him. Not when he'd pushed her there himself.

He moved toward her, but she held up a hand to ward him off, and straightened, tears streaming down her face. He considered that for a brief moment and then he simply took hold of her hand and pulled her into his arms.

"Listen to me," he said, his voice raw. "I can't give you what you deserve. I can't give you anything except tabloid gossip and innuendo, and I hate that. *I hate it*." He shifted her against him, taking her chin in his hand and gently bringing her eyes to his, those melting chocolate eyes, wet and hurt and still the most beautiful he'd ever seen. "But you have to know that I love you, Adriana. I love you and I would never deliberately hurt you. You can trust that, if nothing else. I swear it."

"Pato..." she said, as if his name was a prayer.

"I can't fix this," he told her, the same fury that had ignited in him when he'd seen the papers yesterday surging in him again. That same dark, encompassing rage that had nearly taken him apart. "I can't protect you the way I should. The only thing I can do is let you go." She was shaking her head and he slid his hand from her chin to her soft cheek, holding her there. "You deserve better."

He watched her struggle to take a breath, and she didn't seem to care that her face was wet with tears. She frowned at him.

"And what will you do while I'm out there some-where, finding whatever it is I deserve?" she asked. She shook her head again, decisively. "Martyr yourself?"

"It's not the same thing."

"It's exactly the same thing," she retorted.

"I don't have a choice," he exclaimed. "This doesn't end simply because Lenz marries today. I told you. Thrones are won by treachery. My father will be a threat until he's dead—or until Lenz pro-duces his own heir. Pato the Playboy isn't going anywhere."

Adriana watched him for a moment, then angled herself back to wipe at her eyes. His hand dropped away, and he missed touching her immediately, so much his fingers twitched.

"The Princess Lissette strikes me as highly moti-vated," she said, a hint of that dryness in her voice that he adored, that he knew would haunt him forever. "I give her ten months, maybe a year, before she kicks off the next generation."

"You have to live better than this," he told her softly. "Please."

Adriana looked at him for a long time. He thought she might simply agree, and it would kill him, but he would let her leave him. He had no choice. But then she sighed.

"I thought you told me love was meant to hurt if it mattered," she said, her gaze on his, hard and warm at the same time. "And who's the martyr now? If you order me out of the country, does that mean you can wallow on your own crucifix?"

That dug beneath his skin, straight on into the center of him, making it hard to breathe for a moment. He said her name softly—a warning, or his own version of a prayer? He wasn't sure he could tell.

"Make it real or don't bother calling it love, Pato," she declared, slicing into him with his own words. Daring him. "It *already* hurts. It's *already* painful. What's another year of the same?"

"You don't know what you're saying."

"I'm the one they picked apart the most in those

papers," she reminded him, her eyes gleaming wet again. "I know exactly what I'm saying."

"This has been *one day* of tabloid coverage," he pointed out, determined to make her see reason. "Are you really prepared for the endless onslaught? Day after day after day, until sometimes you wonder if the story they're telling is the truth and you're the lie?"

She moved to him then and put her hands on his chest, leaning into him, making him want nothing more than to hold her close and keep her there forever.

"I have to think that it's better if there's someone else around to tell you which is which," she whispered. "And yesterday was a bad day in the tabloids, but it wasn't the first. I've been a favorite target since I turned sixteen."

Pato couldn't help himself. She was the only one who'd ever seen him, who'd looked straight through all the masks he wore and found him. And she thought he was a good man.

He wanted that. He wanted her. He wanted *this,* however he could have it.

"If you don't go now, Adriana," he warned her, even as he pulled her closer, "I will never let you try again. I will order you to stay with me, and it will ruin you. You will be the most infamous of all the Righettis, worse even than your great-aunt and her disgraced duke. The papers will never let it go. The people will be worse."

She shrugged, but her eyes were tight on his. "Let them say what they want. They do anyway."

"Your friends and family will think you've turned to the dark side," he said, his tone serious, though he could feel his mouth begin to curve, and saw an instant answering spark in her warm gaze. "They will despair of you. They will stage interventions, cut you off, sell secrets and lies to the tabloids and claim you brought it upon yourself."

"I think I love you most of all when you're romantic," she teased, and he could see the smile she tried to hide, even as he soaked in the words he'd wanted to hear again, ever since he'd thrown them back in her face at the cottage. "When you paint me such beautiful pictures of our future. Be still my heart."

But he wasn't done.

"It will be hard and lonely," he promised her. "But when it's done, my brother will sit on that throne, his heir will be hale and hearty and *his,* and I will make you a princess." Pato moved his hands to her head, smoothed back her pretty hair, then tilted her face up. "I will marry you in the great cathedral and make every single one of these Kitzinian hypocrites bow down before you. Our babies will be fat and happy, and know as little as possible of palace life. None of this intrigue. None of these games. And I will make you happy or die trying, I promise you."

"I love you, Pato," she told him, fierce and sure, the truth of it a wild light in her gaze. There was nothing tepid or lukewarm about it, and it burned into him like fire. "I'm not going to give you up." Her mouth curved. "And that means your famous debauchery starts and ends with me. No ambassador's daughters. No nameless former lovers. No *energetic* threesomes."

He grinned. "You think you can handle me all by yourself?"

"Try me," she whispered. "I know how much you like a challenge."

He took her mouth then, hot and hard, making them both shudder. And when he pulled back again, her eyes were shining, and he knew. She was his, at last.

His. For good.

When he let her go again she was smiling, until she glanced at the portraits on the wall and a shadow moved over her face.

"I have to think that someday my family will forgive me for this," she said quietly. "It will hurt them worst of all."

He kissed her again, bringing her attention back to him.

"I suspect they'll find a way to work past the shame," he said, amused, "when their daughter is a princess and the Righetti lands and fortunes are restored to their former glory by an eternally grateful monarch. I suspect they will discover that, secretly, they supported you all along."

Her smile then was like the sun, warm and bright, lighting up all the dark places inside him. Filling in the hollows. He would do the same for her, he vowed. He would take away the darkness. He would bathe her in light until she had no shadows left to haunt her.

He would spend the rest of his life chasing them away, one by one. She was right—he loved a challenge.

"I've never been scandalous *on purpose,*" she said then, as if the idea thrilled her.

Pato laughed. "I've never been anything else. You'll catch on. We can practice at my brother's wedding. I believe we're already late."

"It shouldn't be too hard," she told him, in that way of hers that made him want to lock the door and indulge himself in the perfect taste of her, especially when she looked at him as if she saw nothing but forever in his gaze. Then she smiled. "Rule number seven. I'm a Righetti. Scandal is in my blood."

* * * * *

H.W.